AF605056

TWO CALIFORNIAS

ROBERT GLICK

C&R Press
Conscious & Responsible

Printed in the United States of America

First Edition
1 2 3 4 5 6 7 8 9

Interior design by Jojo Rita

ISBN-13: 978-1-949540-04-8

C&R Press
Conscious & Responsible
www.crpress.org

For special discounted bulk purchases, please contact:
C&R Press sales@crpress.org
Contact info@crpress.org to book events, readings and author signings.

TWO CALIFORNIAS

STORIES

ACKNOWLEDGMENTS

I am deeply grateful to the journals who first published these stories and to the judges who selected them in competitions:

"In the Room / Memory is / White" first appeared in *The Normal School (The Normal School* Normal Prize for fiction, judged by Margot Livesey)

"Release" first appeared in *Passages North*

"Goat Pharmacy" first appeared in *New Orleans Review*

"K/S" first appeared in *Black Warrior Review*

"Hotel Grand Abyss" first appeared in *Copper Nickel (Copper Nickel* Fiction Contest, judged by Ron Carlson)

"Mermaid Anatomy" first appeared in *Notre Dame Review*

"Failure Mechanism (Voicebox)" first appeared in *The Seattle Review*

TABLE OF CONTENTS

"...one has a tendency to see the world as a vast junkyard, looking at a man and seeing only his (potentially) mangled parts, entering a house only to trace the path of the inevitable fire. Therefore when I was installed here, although I knew an error had been made, I countenanced it, I was shrewd; I was aware that there might well be some kind of advantage to be gained from what seemed a disaster."

---Donald Barthelme

I.

IN THE ROOM / MEMORY IS / WHITE

Around the corner from the Mulhouses' adobe-tiled two-bedroom, teenagers hang out on a short, hilly dirt road. It's a few blocks from the high school. When necessary, they retreat behind the dusty scattered white oaks. It is rarely necessary.

Dorian stands at the top of the hill, kicking odd-sized rocks down towards the stop sign. *Crap*, she says to her friends. *Gotta hustle.*

If Dorian's boyfriend is monkey-fingered with matches, she is clumsy with time, and is almost late, again, to take care of Jacob. She gives away the rest of her cigarette. Faint polka dots of ash cover the canary-yellow mailbox next to her.

She has been kidsitting Jacob for two months now; for two months, since the Mulhouses' first *Dine and Debate* night, she has held a vague, low-level worry for him. She likes Jacob, likes how he stretches out her name. She mistrusts Dr. and Mrs. Mulhouse. They overpay her, which is either stupid or arrogant or both. They can ask any of their friends the going rate.

Dorian feels especially uneasy this afternoon. Something's accelerating, becoming smelly, a cheap slab of meat gone bad. Mrs. Mulhouse calls her for *Dine and Debate* nights; never for afternoons. During the day they let Jacob take care of himself.

*

Mrs. Mulhouse wanted to come home before Jacob; she wanted to have a lid-peeled fruit cup waiting for him on the kitchen table, especially since she would barely be able to talk to him before she had to leave again to her appointment. Nonetheless, claiming to have forgotten her purse in her desk drawer, she told her boss, the ophthalmologist, to go on without her. She had just enough time.

Considering she had kicked Dr. Mulhouse out for lying, she looked harshly even upon white lies; she would make herself pay for this one later. But later, she wouldn't be able to compose herself.

She sat herself in the examination chair, lowered the fly machine in front of her eyes, and turned the dials until the room lost focus – grew thick, furry. And further, until she felt a soft gnashing, like an old-fashioned pencil sharpener in her stomach. The nausea comforted her. Then she dialed it back down. Settled into seeing shapes. She felt the stitching in the leather chair. The things she knew stood in front of her, the oversized mason jars of long Q-Tips and eye washes. They were no longer there. They were something else.

*

Dr. Mulhouse leaves work early. He lets his car, a silver BMW, coast down the spiral of the parking garage. A box of Frosted Flakes is belted safely on the passenger seat. The open window sucks in the echoes and muffler pops from the many floors. Parking is $1.15 and he has $1.05 handy and though he has kept his practice in this building for years, the attendant won't let the dime slide. *Is this really fair?* he asks. The attendant, obviously stifled all day in his shack, holds out his hand. Dr. Mulhouse undoes his seat belt, removes his wallet from his back pocket. Above the door hangs the shimmering transparent plastic protecting his dry cleaning. For the last month, he has kept his work clothes in the car.

He wants to staple the attendant's fingers into the slit of the time clock.

He supposes that he should show his anger more often. Like when he found out Jacob had cavities. His rage, what he considered a terrible loss of control, actually made Irene happy. *I'd rather have married a screamer,* she'd said in bed that night, *than a man who shrinks from passion like a dog from an electric fence.*

*

Mrs. Mulhouse made salad. She mixed lettuce, sunflower seeds, and chopped carrots in a big wooden bowl, poured oil and vinegar into what she called cruets. Normally, she and Jacob ate Hamburger Helper with the salad, but tonight Dr. Mulhouse was home. He hadn't been around very much – two days a week, tops.

Jacob watched his mother stuff the crown roast with apples. She was humming, preoccupied; it was a good time to visit the master bedroom. Dr. Mulhouse lounged on his bed, wearing only his underwear and grooved black socks that reached his knees. He was watching the Kings. His favorite was Marcel Dionne. *If there is such a thing as grace,* he once told his son (*And I'm not saying there is,* he said to his wife), *it can only exist on ice.*

Jacob didn't have much time. His mother had been going back and forth from the kitchen to the bedroom, asking Dr. Mulhouse, who was a pediatrician, about chicken pox, or phoning Dorian, who for some reason was coming tomorrow afternoon.

Jacob jumped on the bed. Dr. Mulhouse pulled his son towards him, nestled Jacob in the crook of his arm. Then he picked up a racquetball from the night table and bounced it against Jacob's forehead and Jacob giggled.

Will you take me to the supermarket after dinner? asked Jacob.

Your mother can take you, said Dr. Mulhouse.

Mom can't know! Jacob wanted to buy her a present. An elephant charm.

The Maple Leafs don't have enough gas left in the tank, Dr. Mulhouse said.

Please, will you take me?

What are you getting me?

Jacob didn't answer. Dr. Mulhouse rubbed his hand across his dark sideburns, which had spread in the last month, become more wiry and three-dimensional. *I can't take you tonight*, he said. *And you should buy her a jewelry box. It's cheaper.*

*

Dorian presses the lit doorbell. Her black hair smells of smoke, but she doesn't care. Jacob lets her in.

How's it going, little vole? she says.

Jacob smiles. He's a bit effeminate, with a bowl cut and a kind, round face that makes him seem incapable of that sadistic streak common to ten-year-olds. He comes up close, tracing the futuristic insectoid spaceship on her Journey T-shirt. It doesn't bother her.

I don't know when I'll be back, says Mrs. Mulhouse. She's exceptionally nervous today. The delicate rings on her fingers make her knuckles look gnarly. *Three or four hours perhaps, I don't know.* Gently she pinches the bridge of Jacob's nose and says, *All Cows Eat Grass, okay?* That much Dorian recognizes from music class. She'd been terrible at it – bad ear, choppity rhythm.

How's Dr. Mulhouse? asks Dorian. *I haven't seen him in forever.*

Fine, says Mrs. Mulhouse. *Apparently more kids are sick this year than ever before, he's been forced into scheduling late appointments.*

Jacob demands crab casserole for dinner. *There's Hamburger Helper*, says Mrs. Mulhouse, rolling her eyes. She hugs him and grabs her lipstick off the kitchen table and goes out.

Dorian would swear that Mrs. Mulhouse was about to cry.

*

Jacob took out their World Book Encyclopedia – eight volumes per shelf – to do research on elephants. Some letters didn't merit a single edition. Q, or X. Sometimes, in class, he wished his last name started with Q or X – invisible, too insignificant to warrant attention.

Elephants had big brains and used their ears to cool their blood and the kids had babysitters called allomothers. Jacob laughed. That made Dorian an allomother. He readjusted himself, tilted so that his bare heels were atop the back of the couch, dangerously close to a precarious spoon and two empty Snack Pack puddings. He had the house to himself. Mom was at some appointment.

Some countries, he read, considered white elephants holy. Or good luck. That's what Jacob thought too. He turned back a few pages. The entry on electricity told of a pregnant elephant named Topsy, who was killed by Thomas Edison – he'd been commissioned to electrocute Topsy because Topsy had killed his minder, who had stubbed out cigarettes on poor Topsy's tongue.

*

The outpatient clinic is squat like a bunker – thick concrete pocked with little holes (air bubbles?). It's the type of building her husband calls New Brutalist. Even then, three weeks ago, Mrs. Mulhouse wondered from which dictionary he pulled that ugly term. Now, each time she comes here, she imagines some exotic style of boxing, with diamond knuckles, maybe.

She parks where she can see the entrance/exit to the parking lot, so she can watch for her husband's car in the rear view mirror. She should go in alone, she thinks, double-checking the pads and extra pair of underwear in her purse, and come out alone. It's a powerful way, as her therapist said, to find her footing. She finds that ironic, since finding her footing is proving difficult with her bloated feet.

Just because she kicked him out, she'd told Dr. Mulhouse, didn't mean she didn't want him here. That's what the Crown Roast had meant.

Horizontal jetties of concrete jut out from each floor of the clinic. The workers can look out, but not up or down. Dull dirty concrete blocking the sun. It's depressing. Everyone leaving the building comes out squeaking, in wheelchairs. Three minutes until her appointment.

*

Jacob came up with the idea of the elephant pendant because Dr. Mulhouse had become interested in current events. Each Monday, Jacob had to bring into class an article on some contemporary topic; on Sundays, he and his father pored over the paper. Patiently, using small words, Dr. Mulhouse explained the situation in Cambodia to Jacob, the significance of Kissinger's Africa visit. He mentioned something about greasy Teamsters, and Jacob, with his new left-handed scissors, cut out the corresponding article on steel plants.

He found the ad for the elephant pendant in the metro section: *Pure ivory, with a real Emerald Eye! Only $49.95!* He could afford it; he had been saving for a make-your-own-radio kit.

He could see his mom putting on the necklace. He could feel the halo of a kiss on his forehead. The elephant's watching emerald eye, wise. She would, at that moment, have forgiven him for the television – without even knowing he had broken it. And Dad would stop tiptoeing out at night – when he left, Jacob heard him turning the alarm off, then on again.

*

I don't have much homework left, Jacob says to Dorian. Again he looks at the clock on the oven.

For an hour Jacob and Dorian have been sitting at the Mulhouses' circular dining table, doing homework and nibbling on Oreos. They were out of fruit cups, and Mrs. Mulhouse had forgotten to tell Dorian about Jacob's teeth. Jacob hadn't told her, either. Dorian can hear, despite the glass door to the backyard, the motor of the filtration unit on the Mulhouse's hot tub.

I can finish it later, he adds.

That's not the way it goes, little vole. Besides, I have my own homework.

Dorian tailors every school assignment around a single interesting and obscure topic. This semester, it's Tasmanian devils. History: colonization of Tasmania, desecration of the aboriginal population. Science: quarternary glaciation and edible pods. Today, math: given how many devils are run over by freight trucks yearly, and given reproduction cycles, when will the devil population become endangered?

Dorian puts her eraser on the lazy susan and wheels it around to Jacob. *Thanks*, he mumbles. He has been erasing not an incorrect answer but something he has drawn repeatedly in the margins of his English grammar book.

Thirty minutes later, he catches her eye. *I'm done. Can we go to the supermarket now? I'll give you five dollars.*

You don't need to give me five dollars. Why do you want to go so badly?

I want to buy Mom a present.

If it's for a good cause, she says, *sure, we can go.*

Jacob jumps out of his chair. He puts his foot on the bathroom doorknob, hoists himself up on the door, and maneuvers into a crawl space above his closet. In it stands a two-foot-tall ceramic cobra. Mrs. Mulhouse bought it for him when they took a field trip to Olvera Street. The cobra has a hole in the bottom of its coiled base, plugged by a rubber stopper. Jacob unplugs it, counts and recounts his savings, and climbs back down.

*

Jacob hid in the Jacuzzi. He'd started taking refuge there, with only a few inches of breathing room between the water and the heavy octagonal cover that smelled like a skateboard wheel. He made quiet frog noises that echoed darkly in the narrow band of air. He blew bubbles in the hot stale water. Then, he emerged clean, triumphant, lungs blessed with oxygen, blessed with the perfume from the scattering of bruised persimmons fallen from the tree.

His parents were fighting about the broken television. He had sneaked out through the front door, gone around back, and climbed into the Jacuzzi. They were still fighting, but now they were in the kitchen, arguing about something else.

So, he heard his father yell, *it's all the principle of simplification?*

Not simplification, said his mother. *Common sense.*

It makes no sense. Before this Tricia business, this is exactly what you wanted!

Can you not say her name in this house?

Goddamn stingers!

Did it get you?

Jacob heard the dull shudder of the kitchen's sliding glass door. He pushed up on the Jacuzzi cover with his head until he could see. Dad was trying to smash a wasp with a rolled-up newspaper. The wasp was stupid. Even when avoiding Dr. Mulhouse, it resettled on the same window. Finally his dad killed it.

Good work, said his mother. She had been wiping the crescent under her eyes though she hadn't been crying. She pulled a glass from a cabinet.

Dr. Mulhouse crushed the wasp with the heel of his loafer, picked it up, and threw it outside. *Before then,* he said, pleading, his hand resting on the glass door, *you would have given up everything. Everything. For God's sake, we even tried.*

It was too early then; it's too late now!

Listen to me. This is a gift.

You think your seed is some blessing? She slammed shut the cabinet. The porcelain mugs and wine glasses shook. *You think my body is a crowbar you can use to pry back into this house?*

I won't go in with you.

I'll go myself! Please, I can't fight; I feel like I'm going to throw up. Just leave, okay?

It's not like you're forty, you know. It's not like it would be a mongoloid.

Jacob grew tired from holding the cover. Were they talking about a garden? There was a patch of raspberries Mom was always complaining about. And where was Mom going?

When Jacob's father left for work in the morning, he took a mahogany leather briefcase. On days when he played racquetball, he took a red satchel with white straps. But now, when his mother said *Out!* and his father left, all he took was a box of Frosted Flakes. Leaving Jacob with Raisin Bran.

*

How can such a simple procedure take so long? Since it was illegal when Dr. Mulhouse was in med school, he didn't learn about it, doesn't know how they do it. Still, it seems so crude – scorch the earth, destroy everything. Like beating an egg; the singular, unbroken unit, which he would never one day call Jennifer or Darcy, becomes, under the pressure of fork – or what? a curette? – a clear and yellowish spiral, like a galaxy, and then totally diffuse, what the doctors call terminated.

The receptionist glances at him, turns away. He's sure she has been giving him dirty looks. Perhaps the counselor told the receptionist that when she had asked him how he felt about the matter, he sat there mute, his brow furrowed, until finally Irene said, *Obviously he does not approve.*

He should have lied. Said *Yes, of course, Godspeed to it.*

If he doesn't know what he wants, then how can what comes out of his mouth not be a lie? It's such curious math, he thinks – not having any idea how that phrase came to him – that he wants this life, this marriage, but not this configuration.

What's worse, he has no idea what to change. So he's a liar every word of the way.

The walls are painted blue and pink. Why? It's disgusting for this kind of office. The goldfish sleep behind the small, rust-colored treasure chest. Dr. Mulhouse lets the oxygen bubbles mesmerize him. In groups of two and three, they rise through the tank and, at the surface, explode.

*

Dr. Mulhouse had been away for some days, and when he returned, he found his wife preparing dinner. He touched her lightly on the arm, as if trying not to scare her. *Oh, you're here,* she said, and he replied, *I'm happy to see you,* and she said, preheating the oven, *I don't know if I'm happy or not.* He didn't want to fight. Jacob's door was open, which was unusual; he was cutting a hole in the California on his globe. Evidently the door was already there; Jacob was simply widening it. Why? Some kind of hiding place? Dr. Mulhouse didn't bother him. Let him have his secrets. In the living room he used the remote to turn on the television, but no picture came up. Sound, but no picture. *What the hell?*

What's wrong? asked Mrs. Mulhouse, coming in from the kitchen.

What's wrong? How could you do this?

Do what?

Through Mrs. Mulhouse's therapy sessions, in which her therapist suggested that the separation was actually *profitable to her psyche*, Mrs. Mulhouse taught him about passive-aggressive behavior. This, he thought, turned the tables. A textbook example. *You want to hurt me*, he yelled, *so you break my new television?* He got on his knees behind the television and, inch by inch, examined the power cord for frays. *You destroy my pleasures?*

Are your golf clubs broken? Wouldn't that have been a better target?

In your room! Dr. Mulhouse yelled at Jacob. He had been peeking. Jacob closed his door. Dr. Mulhouse fetched a screwdriver from the kitchen.

What in heaven's name are you doing?

You must have done something to it, he said, unscrewing the television's back plating. She clearly knew nothing about the television, but he couldn't bring himself to apologize. While she was a good wife, at least on some statistical level, every brainless thing he had done was somehow her fault.

Mrs. Mulhouse was in tears. *The casserole's going to burn,* she said. He noticed in his peripheral vision that she was heading to the bathroom. I'm making it sick, he thought. He had already, in his anger, stripped the screw, but he kept digging in.

*

Dorian drives Jacob down the hill in her Nova, from the suburbs into the flats, through the El Salvadoran neighborhood.

She does, in fact, want to go to the supermarket. She loves the supermarket – the free samples and fluorescent lights and lack of flies. It's the cleanest, whitest place in the universe. She knows seven types of apples. And the shopping sprees – what an unexpected bonus. She had planned her next spree for this weekend, but Jacob will need his space, and it will take, as she knows, exactly three minutes.

What's a mongoloid? Jacob asks her. She doesn't know, she tells him, other than maybe someone from Mongolia. After that he says nothing.

It scares her, Jacob this quiet, and it's sabotaging the mental run-through of her planned spree. Never does he offer information on his own, but like a Venus Flytrap, once she says something, he latches onto it. She tries to find out what he's going to buy. *Magic Shell?* He doesn't even shake his head. Nor can she persuade him to play the car game – a game that has never, with other children, failed her. Pointing out the most expensive cars. If a car had a broken headlight, you'd scream Padiddle! for extra imaginary points.

She can see the strip of skin between Jacob's pant leg and his socks. His hands are tightly clasped in the lap of his turquoise corduroy Garanimals. She asks him: *What animal is blue? Whale?* He doesn't say. *Marinated herring?*

If Jacob were her egg, like the unboiled one she had to care for in Home Economics, what would she do? She put her egg in a small basket for strawberries and lined the sides with hay to protect it. It's not her place, but maybe she should say something to Dr. and Mrs. Mulhouse. She would say, I think you need to put more hay in the basket.

They drive past her high school. It's a few blocks off-route, but she loves the flowers surrounding the flagpole: birds of paradise and lilies and dahlias. The marquee says there's a bake sale today. There's time for introspection later, little vole, when you're a teenager. Now's all about tide pools and mud pits and baby geckos, their glorious green scaly bodies, each one latching its tiny teeth around your finger. Now's a time not to look so beaten.

*

Jacob followed Mrs. Mulhouse into the living room. She walked right past the television. She sat on the step of the stone fireplace and looked out into the backyard, where a squirrel once fell dead from an electrical wire and landed on his father's last raspberry plant. He insisted on calling Animal Control to take away the possibly rabid squirrel.

His mother didn't even look at the television. Instead, she sat there with a glass of wine, pinging it with her fingernail.

Jacob closed the bottom half of the Dutch door that opened onto the kitchen. He set a small yellow Nerf ball on the carpet, then kicked it with his bare foot into the open space over the door.

Don't you want to play with your new scissors? she asked. *You seemed to like them.*

Jacob did like them, and he appreciated the fact that his mother didn't really want him to be left-handed. The only other left-handed person in his class was a red-bobbed girl named Tiffany. The class called her *The Artist.* Once she drew a child with a yellow balloon, but the string tied to the child's wrist was an electrical cord and the balloon was the sun. She went steady with Jacob for one day, then called and broke it off. He'd been despondent. His mother, taking his side, said to his father: *An artistic mind has a good chance of shorting out.* Jacob didn't understand that.

I'm doing this now, Jacob said to his mother. He picked up the ball and squeezed it and watched it unsquish.

It's true, you have so many toys.

Jacob set the Nerf ball in a more difficult spot, one that required a lot of lift to clear the corner of a table.

I don't think another toy will solve the problem, she said.

Jacob kicked the ball. It hit the Dutch door's doorknob and, lucky bounce, went through the open space.

Goal, said Mrs. Mulhouse. She kept pinging her glass. The sound was regular, didn't resonate. It was like some kind of timer. Or a countdown on a game show.

*

Only pride and Dr. Mulhouse's steady hand allow Mrs. Mulhouse to reach her car without fainting. She is in that much pain. Despite the anesthetic. It's not just nerve endings, she thinks, it's nerve endings filtered through clots of emotional damage.

They take her car from the medical center. This relieves her. She could rely on her car, even its imperfections – the difficulties in latching the hood, or how the emergency blinker, once on, takes ten minutes to shut off. In his car, she would have kept her eyes closed. Everything about him arouses suspicion.

Here he is, destroying their marriage, and yet he calmly unlocks her car door, so supportive and, in a practical way, wise. Even suggesting that they needed to pick up food for dinner. She hadn't thought of it. How tenderly he helps her into the passenger seat, picks up her legs, one at a time, and sets them in the car.

A man like that – awful and kind – is a man she should learn to hate. But the pain is too intense and vast for her not to accept his help. Pain, she thinks, makes you stupid.

*

Jacob came in through the back. The key to the sliding glass door was hidden in a terracotta pot. Letting himself into the house had once felt exciting, adventurous, but it had become routine. He pulled the ice-cube tray, which looked like a silver canoe, out of the freezer, cracked out the ice cubes, and refilled the tray.

Two weeks before, Mrs. Mulhouse, upon returning from work, had looked at Jacob and gone straight to the television. What had made her suspicious? He didn't know. *It's hot*, she said. *If it's hot, it means you're watching television instead of doing your homework. Is that true?* Jacob shrugged. She used a Kleenex to wipe a smear of makeup from below her eye. *Go to your room*, she said, *I'm too tired to punish you.*

His idea was brilliant. Cold countered heat, fizzled it out.

He arranged the ice cubes atop the television and turned it on and ran back into the kitchen. There, he grabbed two Oreos, which Mom had moved to an upper shelf, and a napkin – he was careful with crumbs, which liked to hide in the carpet. His timing was perfect – the animated intro to *Batman* was just coming on. He loved the boomerangs, the Batcave, but mostly he loved the almost lulling rhythm of the show, the inevitable returns. Batman and Robin would be imperiled early, triumphant late. And the villains? Captured, only to escape again, and again.

He lay on the carpet, on his stomach, propped on his elbows, cupping his head with his hands. The villain was The Black Widow – a stupid episode; it was always stupid if the villain wasn't The Joker or The Riddler or The Penguin. He split an Oreo and licked the cookie, which felt scratchy, like licking the moon.

Soon came the commercials, and he jumped up and ran outside. He had to turn on all the sprinklers before the commercials ended. Even with The Black Widow, he didn't want to miss anything.

When he got back, he saw smoke wafting from the top of the television. It smelled burnt, like the coffee Mom had started to drink. Shit! A few weeks ago, he said it out loud, and Mom got really mad. Mom looked at Dad to say something, but he didn't.

Jacob punched off the knob. Most of the ice had melted, and water dripped into the TV set. He swept the rest of the ice onto the carpet, but the smoke kept coming. The screen was black except for a single bright line across its middle. There was still sound: *That's not the ruby of Mesopotamia*, yelled Robin, *but imitation zircon covered in cherry frosting!*

The ice didn't even do what it was supposed to do – the television was still slightly warm. He climbed onto the kitchen counter and removed the battery from the smoke detector. He opened all the windows. Then, for ten minutes exactly, he stood in his closet, his face pressed against a dark corner.

When he emerged, he tried to read his science book, but he couldn't stop crying and the words were blurry. He kept listening for Mom's car. He kept sniffing the air.

*

Jacob runs towards the supermarket. He almost trips on the curled-up front of the mat that opens the electric doors. Someone shouts at him to walk. The side of the elephant seller's cart is halfway down the long hall, between the checkstands and the supplemental businesses – bank, dry cleaners. There's a florist and a pharmacy on the far side of the cart. He used to like comparing the smell of roses to the smell of rose-scented air fresheners, but now that bores him. He keeps running; he should hurry. Still, he really wants a bag of candy corn. He hasn't been allowed any sweets since he got cavities. He loves the smooth waxy exterior – tri-colored, like a firework lit at night – and the mushy insides.

He wiggles under the turnstile; the idea of the candy corn distracts him. He has memorized everything he can do with candy corn:

- Stick up nose, snort them out
- Make vampire teeth
- Lick them and connect for buildings or picket fences
- Thread needle, make a cannibal necklace
- Rubber band across room
- Melt in microwave
- Push fingers in to see fingerprints

There's a crowd of people surrounding the elephant cart. What if they're sold out of elephants? He ducks back under the turnstile.

*

Before Dr. Mulhouse got dressed, he put the bolsters back on the sofa bed. It was the office of the divorced woman from their *Dine and Debate* group – she freelanced, made architectural drawings. She wouldn't take him in her own room. Even more shamefully, she retreated to her kitchen as soon as her breath had sufficiently slowed. The back door was aslant from the house frame and he had to pull hard to shut it. Behind him, the goddamned wind chimes crashed – he wished she'd tie them up. Of course, if she did, she wouldn't know when he left.

He spent a minute adjusting the mirrors on the loaner car. Last week, rushing from her house, he had backed into a trash can, and now his car was at the repair shop, having its dents hammered. He drove down the canyon, unwrapped a Peppermint Pattie. Soon he got on the freeway. It was foolish and destructive to go straight home from there, but he had no time to take a shower. A few times a week, as per agreement, he came home to have dinner, watch TV with Irene and Jacob, and put Jacob to bed. Then he would go back to his hotel, where they no longer put mints on his pillow; he had to nick them from the front desk.

If only he could explain to Irene why he couldn't break off the affair. The truth was, he didn't know. It wasn't the sex, which, like checkers, simply demanded his attention for a particular period of time. *You made it through med school,* Irene said. *Give that brain of yours a wash and see what comes out.* He wanted to understand, but he only approached clarity when trying, in his head, to explain it to an imaginary older Jacob.

Dear Jacob, he would say to his hotel mirror, *sometimes the gnawing is greater than the quiet satisfactions. Try and resist the gnawing.*

He clicked open the garage door. Mrs. Mulhouse had taken up both spaces. Irritated, he backed up and parked on the street.

Jacob sat at the dinner table, fully occupied with his handheld electronic game, the one where you were a fireman holding a stretcher or a trampoline or a big sheet, and your job was to catch babies thrown from a burning building. Did his son have any idea what was going on? Irene took his coat, as she always did, and draped it neatly over one of the dining room chairs. In part, it was the way she held onto the little rituals, like they were a lifeboat, that made him want to bring his open hand down on a cactus and have the entire family watch him bleed. How could he not know how to change things? The color of blood had nothing to do with oxygen. His would be bright orange, the flame of a gas stove.

Did something happen at work today? asked Irene.

Sure, something happened, he said, not kissing her cheek, *just nothing of interest.*

Dear Jacob, he thought, hotels are expensive and bleak.

*

The supermarket is across the street from the high school Jacob will go to if Dr. and Mrs. Mulhouse don't divorce and Jacob has to move away. It shares space in the mini-mall with old New York chains: Nathan's, with its extra long hot dogs and Coney Island photographs, and HoneyBaked Hams. Honey and ham together? A terrible idea. *Can we get Carvel?* asks Mrs. Mulhouse. She doesn't crave the ice cream – she wants the fake icing shaped like a man's pompadour atop the cakes.

That's not what you should be eating, he says. *You wait in the car.*

Why? she says, opening her door.

Dr. Mulhouse has already picked up her antibiotics, so they walk directly through the pharmacy at one end of the supermarket. The pain radiates in spikes from her cervix. Her left side hurts terribly. Each cramp makes her stop, bend over, clutch herself. Even with a shopping cart, which they don't really need, her gait is limping and uneven.

We shouldn't have, says Dr. Mulhouse. *We made a mistake.*

She waves him off. One by one, they pass through the turnstile. It takes her almost a minute. *Bastard,* she says.

*

When Jacob got home from school, having spent himself running from Morgan Crisp (the class called him Morgan Crispy) during both recesses and lunch, he changed immediately into his Batman swimsuit. The hot tub was luke-warm – the sun had heated the water nicely. Cold water made his toes hurt.

A few nights ago, Mom and Dad had fought for so long that finally he grew bored and closed the door to his room. He took a pillow and a book – *A Wrinkle in Time* – and climbed up into the crawl space. He had fallen asleep there.

Ever since, he made sure to be in the hot tub before Mom got home. He had even cleaned off the thick layer of goopy algae with a broom. Then, to get the goop off the broom, he had to use his fingers.

He used the strap on the underside of the hot tub cover to pull the cover over him. The water reached his lower lip. On the other side of the property wall, the neighbor's Great Dane barked and barked.

Four dead wasps floated in the water – how did they get there? As a game, with one cupped hand, he tried to herd them from point to point. Into the gaping mouth of the filter, but not inside! Next, he split them into two groups of two and, using both hands, raced them from one side of the hot tub to the other.

Then the cover lifted up and sunlight streamed in, making the water oily bright like soap bubbles, and his Mom was standing over him.

He lifted his arm a little out of the water, as if offering it to her. She was going to pull him out and spank him. Even though Coke had now been declared off-limits, he had taken a glass, left it on the table. *Sorry*, he whined.

She kneeled. Dead wasps scattered in slow waves across the water. *Can I come in?* she asked. Clothes and all, she got in and tugged the cover over them. The top of her sleeve floated to the surface. *What do you do in here?*

I don't know.

Are you running away from us?

A wasp drifted towards his mother. Jacob swished it away. *I don't know*, he said again. He wanted to get out, now that it wasn't a secret place any more. And it frightened him, seeing her like this. Still, he liked being with his Mom, liked it being quiet.

You've been so bottled up, she said. *Maybe you should be an artist after all.*

Jacob opened up the cover, folding it back over on itself. He climbed out of the tub. *I'll get you a towel*, he said.

*

In the supermarket, Dorian is content to let Jacob do what he wants. Even if the Mulhouses return early, they still have an hour. Jacob can keep his big secret to himself, and she can run her shopping spree.

Dorian has a thing for *Laverne and Shirley*, and when she saw the episode where they won a contest to go on a shopping spree, she got all her friends to imitate it. Three minutes in a supermarket, what could you bring out? Of course Laverne and Shirley blew it. They got greedy, stuffed their angora sweaters with smoked oysters, and didn't make it across the line, except for one outstretched hand. Shirley lay collapsed on the floor, like an obese, toppled Statue of Liberty, holding a single roll of paper towels.

No way is this going to happen to Dorian. She has devised

a million different routes, based on expense, type of food, the ingredients for recipes she wants her mother to make. Certain aisles she can skip, like the aisle with pet food, but that makes for more intricate cart patterns. Now she's on aisle five. She passes the different meats – slabs, chunks, T-bones, pork chops, roasted and smoked, different types of cut up cow and pig.

What if Dr. and Mrs. Mulhouse just disappeared? Like Amelia Earhart in the Bermuda Triangle. Could she and her boyfriend take care of Jacob?

She's lost track of her route. She overcorrects and cuts a corner too tight, knocking over bottles of barbecue sauce. Precious seconds taken to pick them up. What was next? Capers? No. Fish sticks? Yes. She opens the freezer's fogged doors, pretends to take out a box of Fisherman Jake's Super Breaded. Essential, she reminds herself, to factor the grabbing and fumbling of objects into total time.

*

Dr. Mulhouse drove home from work, from a day during which he saw a toddler bitten by a dog. The parents insisted that he treat the child as if the exclusively indoors dog, a scruffy gray thing with the hiccups, had rabies, which meant that he had to administer an injection in the stomach. The most painful place to receive a needle. The child howled and howled.

On a whim, he drove up the dirt road around the corner from his house. The last scrap of undeveloped land in the entire valley. Even though it was inevitable, outracing the dust the BMW stirred up satisfied him.

For some months, he had actually been trying to get caught. During sex, he had shown Irene new moves, hoping that she would wonder where he learned these things. Not really learned – it was the inevitable physical differences of two different bodies creating different patterns. Irene remarked only that he had been sleeping better. Not snoring, not flailing.

That day, while he'd bounced the child on his knee, wanting more than anything to escape, to treat cleft palates in Nicaragua, he mustered the courage to tell her. If courage meant desperation, he thought. How ironic that one could be so generous to strangers and so terrible to the people one loved. Nixon had made his wife put toothpaste on his toothbrush every morning.

He'd keep it simple – I'm having an affair, he'd say.

The garage door didn't open. He hit the brakes, pushed the button harder, and the door began to rise. He would tell Irene he was sorry, but what he meant to say is that he had to muddy the waters.

Mrs. Mulhouse sat at the dining table, crossing items off long supermarket receipts. On the lazy susan stood the two ugly silver candelabras that Mrs. Mulhouse bought last Christmas, florid angels swirling around the base. She kept her head close to the receipts; she had been complaining of poor eyesight, had asked the ophthalmologist to teach her how to use the machines in the office to analyze herself. Jacob was whimpering, his head turned sideways on the table, as if napping. His little ragmop head.

Your son has cavities, said Mrs. Mulhouse. *Three of them.*

How could you let him get cavities?

Don't blame me, she said. *It's not like I'm letting him eat more junk food. In fact, I'm trying to figure out if I'm buying anything more than usual, but I can't find any discrepancies.*

What do you have to say for yourself? he asked Jacob.

I'm brushing my teeth, Jacob said. This infuriated Dr. Mulhouse. Could no one in this family take responsibility for anything? He wrapped his arm around Jacob's waist and lifted him out of the chair.

Jacob started to hit his father's back. Dr. Mulhouse sensed

that Jacob could hit him harder.

Sometimes people just get cavities, said Mrs. Mulhouse.

One, sure, but not three all at once. Why are you defending him?

As he carried Jacob to his son's room – Dr. Mulhouse didn't like spanking Jacob on his own bed – Jacob screamed directly into his ear; it was more excruciating than a fire-engine siren revolving inside his brain. Mrs. Mulhouse looked horrified, because he hadn't spanked Jacob in years, but he knew she appreciated him taking charge. He would be dispassionate about the spanking. At that moment, he wanted to hurt his wife more than he wanted to hurt his son. No longer would he say: *No, of course I don't care for her.* He would tell Irene: *Guess what? Tricia and I made love during your therapy sessions.*

*

Mrs. Mulhouse digs her thumbs into a package of sirloin, leaves a jagged, bitten nailprint in the plastic. *Still*, she says, *now that that's over, we can tackle only one problem, not a hive of them. Once you complicate things, you can't untangle anything.*

I wouldn't exactly call this a problem, he says.

She picks up a package of hamburger meat. *Why in heaven make a cow look like a burrow of compressed maggots?*

Some girl in the next aisle yells, *Crap!* They hear the rattle of a cart against a shelf. *I thought kids had to be supervised here*, Dr. Mulhouse says.

Only during school hours, says Mrs. Mulhouse.

Flagellate them with Red Ropes, he says, and she gives him a look for making her laugh.

Once the pain subsides, Mrs. Mulhouse puts down the hamburger meat. *Chicken. Or lamb chops with mint jelly.*

Three, he says. *Tonight, for three.*

And then you go wherever you go.

Why? I could sleep on the couch. I could take care of you a little.

You wouldn't sleep on the couch, and I can take care of myself, and I don't want that woman's sloughed cells on me.

That's a dark way to say it.

Are you going to tell me it wasn't a dark thing to do?

How are you feeling?

Not good, she says. *Decision made. Lamb chops it is.*

*

The first night Dorian took care of Jacob, the night Dr. and Mrs. Mulhouse went to their first *Dine and Debate* group, Dr. Mulhouse was friendly, voluble. Holding up a bottle of wine, he quipped that if they came home drunk, it would be from the Aqua Net in the air. Mrs. Mulhouse said she was going for the finger foods, not the politics.

Jacob told her what time he should go to bed. He was drawn to her immediately. He set the alarm himself, told her the code. He drank cups and cups of Coke. It seemed to her that he kept it in his mouth for as long as possible, swishing the syrupy black sugar. She should ask Mrs. Mulhouse about that.

After he fell asleep, she went into the courtyard. It was a funny space, an open-roofed walkway and a small rock garden full of sharp-veined mica between the two front doors. When she tried to read, the green outdoor lights made her nauseous.

She ashed her cigarette in their dustpan. All in all, despite the fact that Mrs. Mulhouse didn't leave written instructions and Dorian had to ask for their phone number in case of emergency, the Mulhouses seemed pleasant enough.

*

Jacob stands in front of the elephant cart. A mannequin holds strands of identical gold necklaces. In the case are, thankfully, three elephant charms in ascending sizes, daisy-chained together, trunk to tail, set against black velvet.

Shyly, out of breath, Jacob asks the man if he can see one of the elephants.

That's a good choice, says the man. *You're young to have such refined tastes.*

He holds the elephant in his palm. It's beautiful and smooth and lucky. Luckier than a bright green rabbit's foot on a keychain. His mother will love it, and she'll stop doing that thing where she twirls a pencil in her hair, which makes her seem so old.

Two grown-ups stand next to Jacob. The seller tells them how tusk charms are selling even faster than the Hawaiian puka-shell necklaces the teenagers love.

As Jacob digs in his pocket for money, he hears, at a distance, his mother's voice. Immediately he senses that she is in pain. He sees her far away, past the checkstands, at the end of an aisle. The way she bends over to put something back on the shelf, how she holds her stomach with one arm and hangs onto the shopping cart.

He can't let her see him with the elephant. He has to give it to her at home. Maybe in a secret ceremony in the hot tub. He pulls his hand out of his pocket – a ten-dollar bill and some change – and throws it down on the glass case before running, elephant in hand, towards the exit. The seller will be angry, but it would take too much time to give him all the money.

Jacob runs past a woman with her jug under the filtered water dispenser. There's the sound of a shopping cart being crushed into the back of the other linked shopping carts in their corral. Jacob pushes the button that opens the trunk of Dorian's car, climbs in, lowers the trunk door over him. The elephant feels like a cookie hidden in his hand. Once he lies down, he's not uncomfortable. It's black and hot and it smells like dry dirt that has been set on fire.

RELEASE

I'm trapped in the middle seat of this middle-aged plane painted to resemble Shamu the killer whale, popping honeyed peanuts into my mouth and contemplating the social significance of zombies. Specifically, I'm breaking down the epic George A. Romero tetralogy; *Night of the Living Dead, Dawn of the Dead, Day of the Dead*, and *Land of the Dead*. Next week I'm presenting a Zombie for Dummies lecture to freshman film students. In preparation, I'm jotting down bullet points on the drink napkin: *they feed on brains, they enjoy spectacular fireworks, they are drawn to the mall because it was an important place to them*. It's not easy to dumb zombies down, but I must admit that I welcome the challenge, a few minutes to gather my thoughts before I see Grandma, barely alive, downgraded to a bleached cotton slip and a diet of Chinese chicken salad. She has been hanging on for three days now, waiting for me to bless her leave.

*

When I was admitted to Berkeley, her rouged cheeks brightened clown-pink with pride, and I glowed at her glowing. She gifted me a super-tech telephone, a phone-answering machine combo that actually spoke. *You have – TWO – new messages*. I programmed her onto the first speed-dial and rang her every Sunday after *Face the Nation*, we gabbed about how her teacher's pension bought her a new cherry-red Thunderbird. One week the phone went kaput, neither power nor dial tone. Illogical, I write on the napkin, that despite their doltishness, zombies manage to cut electricity to the houses they besiege. I didn't want Grandma to think I was careless with her offerings so I wrote an outraged note, express-mailed the phone back to the factory. A month later, I received an unmarked box, the phone sheathed in plastic and ammonia sanitized, and a form letter that said *We regret the fact that this Panasonic warranty does not cover: INFESTATION.* The single word rubber-stamped in red ink. I was living in an anarchist collective, my black-walled room one floor above the vegan kitchen. Naturally I had read Gramsci and was dubious of corporate anything, so I unscrewed the phone's back panel. In the innards I found four perfectly preserved cockroach exoskeletons. Their wings veined, diaphanous, drawn to the hearth of the motor. I excised the tape mechanism and hung it in the collective art gallery, kept the manual and continued to regale Grandma with its preposterous features. I couldn't bear to tell her that her gift had failed me.

*

My stomach has plummeted, we've started our descent, and I will not fail her. She will be lying slack and unconscious under a painting of a woman whose bare skin is the blue of deep sea water. Nonetheless, she will recognize my presence from the particles of dust that orbit slowly around her. Then she will let go and there will be an epiphany of light, the illumination of a suburban house already preparing for her passing, the making museum of spare bedrooms, these rooms which in zombie movies turn into barricaded fortresses, wardrobes shoved up against doors. When you study zombies, you almost never get laid. At dinner parties, I'd unpack *the Marxist implications of the dead's leaderless army.* Tipsily I'd sidle up to cute girls and tell them about my dissertation, the snappily titled *Zombie Renaissance: Divining Intestines in a Post-Capital Dystopia.* It functioned poorly as an icebreaker, the girls more amused than beguiled. I considered a topic shift to vampires but quickly grew bored with the overwrought perfection of immortality. Vampire punctures delicate, their iconography ornate. As if zombies were some kind of home, I came back to their call. I was fascinated by them. In the pantheon of the undead, only zombies give uncensored insight into the transitional space between life, death, and rebirth. Even if you're lucky enough to watch someone die, the life cycle is all hacked up, an arrowhead more than a circle. If you're not as fortunate, if your twin brother Andy had spent fourteen years in a coma, and you hadn't seen him once since you felt him go stale in your arms, and if your parents didn't tell you he had finally died until two weeks after, then natural conceptions of growth and decay are even more hopelessly fragmented. It's a miracle I don't compensate by breeding indiscriminately. In contrast, when humans are infected by zombies, you're afforded the precious opportunity to witness their return. Their eyeball may be uncoiled and boinging upside the socket, so what? You can still be liberated simply by witnessing this uninterrupted sequence. Inexorably, death leads to the zombie's tottering next step, that's why born-agains hate zombies. Because they chew at the barbed wire dividing life and death. Like the trailer says, *when there's no more room in hell, the dead will walk the earth.* My ears just popped, the sorority girl in the Cal sweatshirt is folding a stick of Juicy Fruit into her mouth, does she offer me one? Like I said, there's no love for our kind, probably because I have slipped her drink napkin out from under her orange juice and scrawled: *Every dead body that is not exterminated becomes one of them! It gets up and kills! The people it kills get up and kill!* The ink on the napkin overlays a map of America, the arc of flight routes looks like the migration of a virus, and the body cannot, not without help, sever itself from the brain. Hang on, Grams, hang on.

*

Unseen peril in the dark, the flying coffin nearly clipping the canine peaks of the Tehachapis. Though undoubtedly he will not come to the airport, I am descending dangerously close to my father. He who couldn't possibly seek shelter further from his heart, he who tallies one son dead and the other estranged. Here's our average convo: *Hi,* I say, *it's me.* He says, *I'll get your mother.* I last saw him three years ago, at Andy's funeral; we had just turned twenty. It was a blistering and blue-skied morning, a magnificent brightness that unnerved me the same way that people visit Auschwitz with the expectation of thunderstorms. Instead they feel warm sun on their skin, daffodil fluff floating pacific around them, and they interpret their discomfort as survivor's guilt. There should really be a movie about Holocaust victims who return as zombies to wreak revenge on the Reich. If there's a movie called *Zombie Ninja Gangbangers,* then anything is possible. Before the funeral even started, Andy's nurses, stumpy women with glinty crosses and Kmart smocks, were weeping in the back row like a goddamned Greek chorus. They pissed me off for three reasons. One, they wailed like they knew him more intimately than I did. Two, they did. And three, they were sanding down my extreme resolve not to cry. I didn't want to cry because Mom had been crying ever since Andy's accident, as if his coma had dammed up her life and all that could sneak through was this crack, this leak of tears. Besides, it was completely ridiculous, having a funeral for someone so long on life support, not to blaspheme but he'd been dead for a while. I was dissociating once again on Dad's untucked shirt and Grandma's manicured nails. She sat next to me, dressed in silk and silver pearls; a Bette Davis, black widow kind of look. During the service she whimpered in an overly dramatic way that I couldn't really fathom. I patted her hand. This, of all things, interrupted Mom's crying enough to provoke a mean, disbelieving stare that I didn't understand either. The bitter and the despondent at war in Mom's smeary, large-pored face. I was rooting for the bitter. Wrath, if all went well, might move something. I adjusted my tortoise shell glasses. Rabbi Frehling was finishing off the Kaddish, *aleynu v'al kohl yisrael v'eimru Amen.* Grandma stood up, her calves buckled, it didn't surprise me that she crumpled to the immaculate grass. Dad had prepped me with smelling salts and I snapped them under her nostrils. He towered over her, disgust seeping out of him like garlic, Grandma in involuntary, quivering reflex. Then she came to. *Where am I, where am I?* Dad was yelling, *You won't be satisfied unless you're the star!* I helped Grandma to her feet, focused on the gleaming brass drawer handles in the wall crypts that backdropped the funeral. I unrecline my airplane seat and wonder exactly how zombies break out of wall crypts. Are there catches on the inside, like the anti-kidnapping latches in the trunks of new cars, or can zombies bust out of them like Uma Thurman in *Kill Bill II*? By this time Dad had disappeared behind the acacia gardens to let off steam and Mom had with an unforgiving hand led Grandma away and everyone else had trudged sadly to their sedans, it was just me and Andy and the groundskeeper collapsing chairs. I walked over to Andy's coffin, my clip-on tie weighted down with sweat. *This is going to have to pass for goodbye*, I said, running my hand along the unfinished pine coffin. My fingers gathering splinters. I apologized for not saving him, for not watching him grow up, for not being at his deathbed. A blinking red light in peripheral vision; Dad's fancy video camera taping his own son's funeral. It's then that I started to cry. I despised his patchy stubble, the stains under his armpits. Shame, pathetic and muddy brown, because our arsenal against grief was so paltry, the sunglasses and the camera and the pine box between my twin and his suitors. The groundskeeper coughed. I went and pocketed the videotape, the groundskeeper rolled Andy towards the mausoleum, the stewardesses are strapping themselves backwards into their chairs. Electronic devices should, by force if necessary, be switched off.

*

Sure enough, only one parent picks me up at the airport. Mom doesn't pull out from the parking spot until I fasten my seatbelt, safety being Mom's number one priority. That's why we drive to Grandma's house in a baby blue Volvo. Every so often, when Mom's not glancing fretfully into the rear view mirror, she shifts her eyes my way, probably to see if I've lost weight, her brittle lashes blinking and blinking. She doesn't speak, I don't help her out. My hands are clutched in my lap, the uneasy silence preferable to a chuckling assessment of Grandma's charms or a histrionic attempt at parent-child bonding. We pass the Disney studios: a 30-foot tall Mickey Mouse helium balloon tethered to a parking lot by bright red ropes. *You know Walt got frozen*, I say. My voice weirdly accusatory. Mom replies, *That's an urban legend.* I say, *No, he's beneath Disneyland, in a fucking cryogenic box, right below the Pirates of the Caribbean.* She accelerates onto the 134, stays in the slow lane. I look out my window, at the Priuses with their bumper stickers that say *My father went to the Republican National Convention and all he got me was this lousy white cowl.* I'm trying to wrap my head around why she so ferociously caretakes my innocence with her omissions, never having brought me on her weekly trips to visit Andy, not telling me about Grandma's imminent demise until four hours ago. It makes no sense, as if by protecting me I wouldn't share her unnatural attachment to him. As if she innately understood that zombie children are the most dangerous. Their stunted growth capitalizes on your sympathies, you allow them close and they nip deadly at your ankles. Mom says, *Grandma would have liked us to get her one of those boxes.* Her sniffling flares her capillaried nostrils. *That's not out of nowhere,* I say. Mom shakes her head. It's clearly a sequitur, and the fact that I don't get it has enraged her. Suddenly she swipes the station wagon onto the freeway shoulder, she hasn't been this angry at me since I was seven. It was a few months after Andy's accident, after another operation had left him caved in, without the bones on one side of his skull. She had just returned from the hospital to drive carpool and I started a spit war with my classmates and she pulled the Vista Cruiser station wagon over by an emergency call box. This time she slams on the brakes and in the front seat we jerk forward together. *Do you know what she thought?* she screams. *She thought that she could keep all disease away from her! She thought if she didn't think about death she would never die!* I reply, *So?* My voice has a *what's your problem?* sound to it. *In Ayurvedic medicine, if you never drink milk, you'll never be stung by mosquitoes. Maybe it's the same.* Mom cries, *It's not the same! It's not the same!* I say, *Look*, not wanting to get into it, *she didn't like spiders either, not even daddy long-legs! She didn't like anything creepy, can you really blame her for that? It's how she was.* Mom reaches for a Kleenex from a flowery box. Her voice is an acidic shrill: *Not once did Grandma come to see Andy in the hospital! Not once!* A remarkably straight vein pulses from Mom's temple down to her jaw. She glares at me, waiting for sympathy or solidarity. I return her gaze with as much flare-eyed resentment as I can muster. *Just take me to her, okay?* I roll down the window, push my head into the smog, remembering the year after the accident. Maybe Mom and Dad were trying to conceive a replacement child and had no time for my phonics lessons, they pawned me onto Grandma and she took me to Manhattan. She had me stand atop the toilet seat in my aunt's apartment. There, out the bathroom window, stood the Empire State Building, lit up red white and blue like a popsicle. Majestic, sparkling. Grandma's fingers curled protectively in the belt loops of my orange corduroy pants. In the baby blue Volvo I feel a vertiginous sensation like standing up too quickly but immensely pleasurable. Sullenly Mom blows her nose, her hands locked at ten and two on the steering wheel. She crashes back into traffic, driving with a recklessness utterly new to her. My sniffling nostrils suck in the stink of oleander, the black-leaved plant that soundproofs the sides of freeways, a plant whose sole purpose is to absorb what is toxic and corrosive in this world.

*

The stairs up to Grandma's house are cracked by tree roots. Mom walks behind me, shuffling through the mail; social security payments and gardening crews. I am not ready to let Grandma go. Everything in me wants escape, mindless immersion in the most juvenile contradictions of zombie life, like why do zombies eat brains? They can't die of starvation or thirst, they don't require 2000 calories per day, so what's with the food requirements? Mom has to prod me before I bang the horseshoe-shaped knocker against the door. Dad lets me in, gives me a perfunctory once-over, no change in these disappeared years to his muppet eyebrows and hunched shoulders. I walk by him without saying hello, into a living room full of Louis XIV and slender sculptures of naked women. Mom sits herself primly down on a piano bench; I guess they don't kiss when in crisis. *Her heart is failing,* Dad says, sighing out each word as if reticent to burn energy on me. *And there's fluid backing up in her lungs.* He's wearing a red Izod shirt, collar dusted with dandruff. *Which means?* I ask. *Basically, she's drowning.* I walk down the hall. Dad says, *Nice talking to you.* The house doesn't smell of old people. It smells worse, unchanged, still the sweet lavender from the French soaps in the guest bathroom, the smell of pears. I make the turn into Grandma's well-lit room.

*

She looks so shrunken and animal now. I smile, because I am here, though her eyes are closed and a terrible sound is gurgling from inside her. Each shallow exhale bubbles up like a percolator. I reach the edge of the bed, slide my hand under her chalky fingertips. Already she's crumbling to dust. I wait for her to acknowledge my presence, for her bony shoulder to ripple some notation, for her filmy eyelids to twitch. In the backyard there's the paint-faded totem pole that I used to slam into, head-first, at full speed, to try and bring Andy's coma upon myself. In the living room, Dad's voice has piped up an octave; he's haranguing Mom about coffin costs. I hear Mom *ssssh!* him. For some minutes I wait. When Grandma does not give me a sign, I whisper, *I'm with you now. I'm grateful for everything you did for me, did you know you saved me?* I think I feel her relax, her body settling imperceptibly into the sheet, and this brings me endless joy; it's a terrible time for Mom and Dad to stomp back in. I crane my head around. For fuck's sake, Mom's drinking a Diet Coke, looking demurely at the carpet. Dad says, *It might take a day or two, I'll stay here tonight,* but obviously Grandma's ready to die. She's shutting down. Dad knows it too, I can tell he's lying by the way he mines his ear for wax. I say, *I just got here.* He says *Johnny,* as if he must make me diminutive, *you should go home with Mom.* I give him a skeptical look, one eyebrow up. *I promise,* he adds. Dig, dig, digging into his ear. *She'll still be around tomorrow.* I hear the heavy water bubbling in Grandma's lungs. *I'm not going anywhere,* I say. *What,* whines Dad, *you're going to go on strike? You're going to chain yourself to the bed?* Mom says, *The ficus needs watering.* She takes her color coded keys from her purse and leaves the room. I force myself to breathe, as if the air is so stagnant that it can no longer move into my lungs. *You don't get it,* I say to Dad, *I want to be here.* Outside, the hummingbirds are twitting at the sugar water in the feeder, they peck at the blood-colored liquid with their beaks and pull back so sharply they have to rebalance their claws on the feeder's edge. *Johnny!* yells Dad. He actually stamps his foot but it's an impotent thud. I get now that he is desperate, he needs her all to himself. Soon she will turn, and he knows that zombies inevitably betray those who loved them in life, they leave us behind. We are no longer able to prove ourselves worthy of their love, yet we believe they can still redeem us; this makes us reckless to regain our humanity in the maggoty face of their disappointments. *Please,* my father says. His palms are open and tremoring. It shocks me, but I feel compassion for him, I don't belittle his tyrant shtick. *Fine,* I tell him, *I'll go home.* It's like a gift, the brokenness instantly drains out of him. *Goodbye,* I say to Grandma. I kiss her cheek, feel her wrinkles on my lips, breathe in her parchment smell. Grandma with her gaunt skull and shrewd nose, everything spiteful and gorgeous and almost gone. I am about to whisper into her ear, *It's okay, you can go, I release you,* but I can't, I won't. She is not mine to release.

GOAT PHARMACY

I passed my driving test, and Monkeyfur scored me this job at Gaynor Pharmacy. We worked on alternate days, after wrestling practice, bloated on Gatorade. Monkeyfur, who took fourth at the state championships last year, had Tuesdays and Thursdays. I agreed to do the Wednesday and Saturday shifts, allowing Monkeyfur to attend an optional weekend practice. It wasn't much of a sacrifice. I, wrestling at 160, didn't have the talent to make varsity. Coach said I had to improve my reversals. He had full-body alopecia. If we didn't want to run extra tapeline sprints, we didn't ask to borrow his hairbrush.

Because Monkeyfur kept falling behind on his deliveries (due to having sex in his treehouse with Ginny), Goat had placed both of us on probation. So when I came in on Wednesday, I immediately made sure the back office was clean. Any tiny potatoes mess-up, like an unplunged toilet or a stale 3 Musketeers bar, gave Goat a legitimate reason to fire us.

To his credit, Monkeyfur had picked up all the packing peanuts, and had even scrawled a note for me: GBS 8.2. Meaning Goat, nastily hung over, might make me mop out the dumpster – he claimed that wet cardboard cultivated fast-developing, drug-resistant toxic molds. Or, applying his flaccid energies to a week's worth of unsold Jumble Words, he might give me little more than a grunt and a nod.

I turned on the transistor radio. Dead or Alive's "You Spin Me Round (Like A Record)" was on KROQ. What did that mean, to have someone spin you round like a record?

Tearing receipts and prescription instructions off a dot-matrix printer, I found that, luckily, I had only two deliveries: Mrs. Bialetti, and the San Gabriel Valley Elder Care Center, what me and Monkeyfur meanly called the *Corpse Preparation Zone.* With my calligraphic pen (in Japan, you wrote your résumé in calligraphy), I copied the delivery destinations onto white paper bags, set the amber-colored bottles into the bags, and dropped the bags into a basket I had, on a dare from Monkeyfur, stolen from Gemco.

Goat stood at the counter. Before I tried to pass him, I offered a small prayer to the *kami* that granted ninja invisibility. The prayer was unsuccessful. "Ari," he said to me, using Monkeyfur's real name, "didn't sweep the front yesterday. He knows to sweep."

As always (when Goat was sober), his long silver hair was combed neatly back from his widow's peak. He wore a brown pharmacy smock; his name, Jim Gaynor, stitched in thread over the pocket. The smock barely circled his gut. He must have weighed 280 pounds – I often imagined him stepping onto the four-pound postage scale and the dial going around 70 times. I guessed him into his late sixties; nevertheless he seemed older, ancient and barely bipedal, with this giant capillaried nose, like the Amazon River Delta seen from an airplane.

"I'll sweep later," I told him politely.

"Donny!" he said, charading the motion of brushing dirt into a pan. "You'll sweep right now." He looked slightly sad. Ever since we agreed on the school's right to conduct random locker searches, he seemed hesitant to chastise me. He gave me a ten-cent raise. My maturity, he claimed, let me provide superior customer service to the aged.

I used the broom to whack dust off the front mat, gave the front sidewalk a cursory sweep, and came back in. Michele, the cashier, stopped dusting off bottles of nail polish and hobbled over to me on crutches. Someone had body-slammed her at a thrash show last week and green-sticked her fibula against a fire extinguisher. She wasn't pretty; teased black hair, zitty, too much turquoise eye shadow. Today she wore blue jeans with spider web embroidery and a bootlegged Mötley Crüe *Theatre of Pain* tour jersey.

"You wannabe new-ro," she sighed, "slow down on the Sun-in." My hair, sculpted down into a sharp point between my eyes, glinted an unnatural shade of reddish-blond.

"What's that scribbling on your skin there?" she added.

"Birthmark."

"It looks remarkably like ink."

"Can I go now?" I asked Goat.

"Take a candy bar," he said with grandfatherly kindness. Michele rolled her eyes. I grabbed a Butterfinger.

Me and Monkeyfur went on deliveries with the Goat Pharmacy truck because Goat was too Scrooge to insure my Toyota or Monkeyfur's convertible black Rabbit. It was Monkeyfur's second Rabbit; he had totaled the first one. After he won our league last year, pinning this dude from San Dimas with a phenomenally fast cradle, his father bought him another, plus subwoofers and tinted windows.

On the way out of the parking lot, the undercarriage of the truck scraped the ground. The rear view mirror showed Goat skulking down the alley to the bar. I put on my right turn signal, as if going to the CPZ. I didn't turn right, though. Instead, I turned left, to Ginny's new house. I couldn't believe she had invited me over. In lit class today, listening to a scratchy recording of *Othello,* she had written her address on my arm. She drew purple daisies to dot her *i's*. Even now, I could feel the softness of her thumb on my skin. Perhaps we would only watch *The Young and the Restless,* which she recorded every day, but I doubted it.

For once, the air wasn't pink and purple and particulate. It smelled almost salty. At red lights, I checked my molars for stuck bits of that hard orange nougat. "I Still Haven't Found What I'm

Looking For" came on the radio. The big sky, the lonely desert. Wanting to be alone, and wanting not to be alone.

In the foothills, I passed unfinished tract homes dressed in astronaut-silver sheets of insulation. The front yards gridded out with squares of raw dirt, the roofs covered in curved, salmon-colored adobe tiles, like sign language for waves. Like the neighborhood in *E.T.* I parked behind Ginny's green Karmann Ghia, opened the glove compartment, and pulled out a rubber. I thought about porn stars. Porn star men had hairy chests and I didn't. The women had big boobs, whereas Ginny had pretty much negative boob. Unless they hid under those baggy clothes she wore, sweaters that hung down to her knees.

I took out a second rubber.

The thatched doormat said *Blessings To All.* Did Ginny really want to make out with me? Was this some perverted test orchestrated by Monkeyfur? Like when he convinced me to hide eviscerated trout in the *cold-blooded vertebrates and fishes* section of the school library.

The samurai code (I wanted to attend a senior exchange program to Kyoto next year. I loved Japan, and had been boning up on all things Nipponesque) said you could either be flogged or pilloried for messing around with your best friend's girlfriend. I didn't care. I rang the bell.

*

I met Monkeyfur two years ago, on Yom Kippur. My Mom had run off with some guy who had macho arm hair like Captain Stubing on the *Love Boat*, and my Dad had moved me to this sewage runoff of Los Angeles. Between the fall and spring semesters of ninth grade. I didn't talk to him for months.

The services at the synagogue dragged on. Everyone prayed about hearing but not really hearing, seeing but not really seeing. During the Torah service, Monkeyfur pulled me out of my chair. I didn't argue, and Dad probably figured that I needed a friend a bit more than I needed a God who let 690-year-old people fornicate.

We walked with a few other guys to Dunkin Donuts. I bought a chocolate cruller, Monkeyfur ate a bear claw. The back lot reeked of lard and weed and wet coffee grounds. Monkeyfur procured a purple bong from the inside pocket of his corduroy suit. The bong made a few rounds, with people coughing and me taking half-lungs to not embarrass myself. Monkeyfur said: "Okay: there's a golden goose in a glass box. There's a hole in the box just big enough for the goose's neck. How do you get the goose out without breaking the box or killing the goose?"

We made up stupid answers. Some guy who had forgotten to take off his *kipah* asked if he could starve the goose.

Monkeyfur said: "The answer is: there, it's out."

"Impossible," I said.

"It's a koan. Either you're a Zen master and you get it or you're not and you don't."

In my hazy state, I made myself remember to look up Zen in the dictionary.

We stumbled back to the synagogue. One of the adults said: "Ari, you smell like smoke."

Ari said: "Must be the new guy."

The man laughed. I laughed. Monkeyfur liked me enough to incriminate me.

*

Ginny was gorgeous. Her white strapless top went great against her skin.

"You've got birds?" I asked.

She closed the front door behind me. "Parakeets. Twiggy

and Eyelash."

"Is anyone home?"

"What do you think?"

Awkwardly I leaned forward and kissed her. Her lips were soft and chapped at the same time. She tasted like wintergreen. "Don't be all crazy," she said, taking my finger in her mouth. I had never felt anything remotely like it.

She led me up the stairs, which felt sticky with gravitational pull. The background in her family photos didn't look like America. Wetback, she once told me, meant anyone who sacrificed everything for a better life.

"Sorry," she said, "my room's kind of messy."

A crucifix was nailed directly on top of the door's peephole.

"It doesn't look messy," I said.

Her room looked nothing like my room. Above my bed hung an original poster of *Mothra*; inelegant, Japanese nonetheless. She had tacked to her wall a collage of her favorite bands: Oingo Boingo, Devo, and The Germs, though The Germs were punk. On her dresser lay a mirrored platform with perfumes in fancy shapes. Yellow and green tassels (our school colors) on the brass bedposts. And teddy bears covered the bed, which disturbed me far more than the photo of her and Monkeyfur from this year's Sadie Hawkins Dance.

Ginny closed the shutters. We kissed some more, bouncing a little bit on the bed's white comforter. She pulled off my collared shirt, slid her hand under my jeans, her nails running lightly through my pubes. My skin there jumped. I tried to distract myself by measuring out the size of her room in *tatami* mats. 6 ½ or 7, I thought.

Still, no amount of thinking about other stuff helped. She licked the outside of my ear, the inside. In the warmth of her tongue, I heard the echo of a conch shell. I felt my muscles tighten around my tailbone, and I came.

This mortified me. So she couldn't tell, I rolled her over. A bear fell off the bed. I pinched her nipples. "Intense," she said. I lifted up her shirt. The arc of her protruding ribs, the sharp crease of her hips, the starburst of raised scars above her belly button. The scars were old; she had sworn to both me and Monkeyfur that she had stopped cutting.

She put her top back down, slid off her bright purple leggings, and placed my hand on her underwear. "Go there," she said.

First, I licked her over her underwear. "Panties," she said. I tugged them down to her knees. I'd never seen a girl's parts up close. She had dark pubic hair, and two flaps of almost swollen skin. To my surprise, I liked the taste, which was indescribable, like *umami.* I couldn't detect a relationship between my tongue and her breathing, and I didn't care. She seemed happy, which made me happy. Every once in a while, I removed the point of my wet Flock of Seagulls hair from my mouth.

"Jesus," she said. Her stomach shuddered. I looked up to see her head haloed by bears. Had she given each one a name, like Princess or Silky?

I felt myself hard again; I had, I realized, been grinding my crotch into the mattress. "I'm going to get a rubber," I said.

"If you want."

My hands shook and I couldn't rip open the wrapper and at first I put on the condom upside-down. I no longer recognized my dick. It was some kind of external attachment, like the crevice tool for a vacuum cleaner.

This is the end of virginity, I thought.

I opened Ginny's closet door.

"What are you doing?" she asked.

Seeing nothing of interest, I closed it. Trying to move in an erotic way, trying not to crush her under my weight, I climbed on top of her. I pretended that I was doing some *kama sutra* thing, sliding myself around her outside skin. The principle, I assumed, worked something like magnets, or suction.

In any case, until I saw her face wrinkle up, it felt incredible.

"Off!" she said. As if giving a command to a humping dog.

"What's wrong?"

We lay there, side by side, on our backs, only our arms touching. Ginny seemed angry and far away, beyond words. Then she bit my neck.

"What the fuck?"

"You're going to be one of those boys," she sneered, "that you have to guide in."

She went to the bathroom. I heard her lock the push-button as well as the bolt. It worried me that she turned on the faucet full-bore, that she was using noise to cover her cutting again.

I waited for her to calm down. After a few minutes, I figured out that she had, in fact, turned on the bathtub. She wasn't coming out until I left. Forlornly I put on my clothes. My neck throbbed. The birds wouldn't stop chirping. As revenge, I thought about hanging the condom in their cage, but I knew how guilty I would feel if one of them choked. And if her parents found the condom, they would blame Monkeyfur; I would feel guilty for that too.

I slammed the front door, for no reason other than to let Ginny know I had gone.

*

When I was eleven, the teacher of my Hebrew class planned an after-school field trip to the Tarzana Convalescent Home. I convinced Mom, who signed the consent form, to give me extra allowance for the post-trip Israeli dinner at Sabra.

I, however, had no intention of going. With the exception of my very sprightly grandma (my other three grandparents had died before I was born), I had a total horror of old people.

My grandma wore a tan leotard everywhere. She did jazzercise in a portable geodesic dome in the back yard of her ramshackle house. Circular saw blades were nailed onto the property fence.

Besides, I couldn't stand the lies my teacher told us about our *mitzvah*. A choir of pubescent kids with cracking voices, singing songs in a language we could barely pronounce, to people who could barely hear; what kind of good deed was that?

That afternoon, I rode my Schwinn cruiser home, changed into my baseball uniform: white stirrup pants, orange jersey with tiny air holes. Because practice was in Studio City, and arranging a carpool would have alerted Mom, I took the public bus down Ventura, sitting nervously between two maids who carried their cleaning supplies in plastic buckets.

My coach didn't like my strike zone; I kept swinging at bad pitches.

That night, Mom found the consent form in the back pocket of my school pants.

"Mrs. Sodokoff didn't ask for it," I said.

"Mrs. Sodokoff is absent-minded. What songs did you sing?"

"*Bashana Haba'ah*," I lied. Mom knew, didn't push. I hid my soiled stirrups under my mattress. After the next game, I buried them at the bottom of the laundry hamper.

*

It was abnormal. Mrs. Bialetti stood there in her front yard, shivering, underdressed. Usually I had to ring three times before she croaked through the intercom, "No more life insurance!" Only when I gave her the secret code – Diclofenac, the name of her arthritis medication – did she let me in.

I parked the truck, leaned over to the passenger seat for her medications; the emergency brake jabbed into my stomach, which felt wrung tight, like a towel at a car wash. My neck still ached. And I wanted to remove the rubber as soon as possible.

Walking up to Mrs. Bialetti, I saw that her knees bowed inwards, as if she had to pee. She wore a sky-blue shirt and white polyester pants that in grade school we called floods; clothing for the pitch and putt.

"I locked myself up," she said.

I groaned. The saurian eyelids and pinhole memories and unthrottled leakages of old people repulsed me. Her blue-green veins stuck out, as if filled with formaldehyde. They reminded me of a science experiment, which reminded me of Mr. Sneek, the body-building chemistry teacher who wore a He-Man doll around his neck. Once, during detention, he made me and Ginny and Monkeyfur watch *Pumping Iron*, in which Arnold Schwarzenegger bragged about how he would rather lift weights than shoot his wad.

"Don't you have an extra key?" I asked. "What about under the welcome mat?"

"You can tunnel in through the doggie door."

Briefly I considered leaving her out to freeze; a Mrs. Bialetti ice mummy.

"Sure," I said. In the end, I didn't despise her. She told me cool war stories about her dead husband, one of the original Flying Tigers, the first ace to paint a shark on his fighter plane.

Having a wrestler's body, thick-kneed and broad-shouldered, it took some time to sausage myself through the doggy door. The door's metal frame caught on my belt. I couldn't wiggle back out, and I had never asked Mrs. Bialetti if she owned a dog. I didn't hear any growling. What if she had a Doberman with no vocal chords?

Cautiously I crawled into the kitchen. On a dusty rosewood end table, a pyramid of pears, mottled brown and concave with rot, sat in a fruit dish. Next to the dish were Mrs. Bialetti's keys. A crinkly handwritten sign wedged into the molding of a pane of stained glass said: *Mom, have you remembered your keys?*

As silver lining, I had an opportunity to take off the condom. It looked pathetic on me, like a talc-colored sea cucumber. I threw it in the trash, covered it with a paper towel, and opened the front door.

"You're my sweet bean," she said. Slowly she raised her arms; she wanted to give me a hug. I was sure I would retch if she touched me. Like on my 15th birthday party, when I got food poisoning from the hibachi shrimp at Shibuya Sushi.

How bad would it be to give her a hug? Would it be a mitzvah? At least Mrs. Bialetti wore clothes. Her parts were the same as any other woman's, even the same as Ginny's, only more dilapidated.

I snatched the money from her hand and left.

As I got into my car, I saw Mrs. Bialetti following me down the walk, one leg dragging behind her; most likely she was getting the mail. I drove away, feeling stupid and ashamed. How infantile, so easily nauseated by the elderly, their drool stains and shit smears. Maybe that explained why Ginny rejected me. Monkeyfur was agile and unafraid and rock-hard and he claimed it was far more challenging to get an F+ than to get an A. I hid behind the couch each time *The Wizard of Oz* came on.

*

About a year ago, before Ginny and I got to know each other, we were named Sophomores of the Month. I didn't do anything special, other than washing the most cars at a fundraiser for Muscular Dystrophy. Monkeyfur stayed home that morning, mimosa in hand, playing shuffleboard by the pool with a stack of stuck-together frozen pancakes.

The school honored us at an Elks Club breakfast held in a bowling alley. I ate crispy bacon and scrambled eggs drowned in grape jelly. Ginny sat on the other side of her Dad, Mr. Menendez, who also happened to be the Dean of Boys. She responded to his questions with curt, resentful nods.

Mr. Menendez presented us with our awards: two free frames each (shoe rental inclusive) and a 25-dollar gift certificate to Tower Records. Ginny's gigantic round eyes seemed to absorb all the light in the room. She chewed on a Chiclet; I loved the sound she made spitting it into the trash. Always she wore mint-green fingernail polish. Everything about her was minty.

The next semester, Monkeyfur and Ginny and I shared a table in Mr. Sneek's class. We concocted our own fire extinguishing fluid and cheated on multiple-choice tests by patterns of winking and blinking. For lunch at Ginny's old house, we deliberately overcooked our microwave burritos, exploding wet beans and liquid cheese against the glass.

One night, at a school basketball game (our beloved Huskies down eighteen by the half), the three of us snuck under the bleachers, inebriating ourselves on Crystal Light and vodka. With Ginny cheering us on, me and Monkeyfur wrestled *sumo* until he gave me a wedgie and I bashed my arm on a piece of metal scaffolding. Vaguely I remembered that I forgotten my trig book; I stumbled to my locker. On my way back, behind the gym, I saw them making out, Ginny's thin body cushioned against an unused blocking dummy.

"That's sick!" I yelled to Ginny. "His whole body's a toupée!"

(As early as 8th grade, Monkeyfur had a mega-hairy back. Someone decided to call him a Sasquatch. Then someone else called him a hairball. A third person noted that hairballs were duh, internal. Sasquatch -> Hairball -> Furball -> Monkeyfur.)

Monkeyfur wiggled his tongue at me a là Gene Simmons.

"You're wasted," Ginny said. "Go home."

Because Monkeyfur's Dad was in Haiti, attending a conference about the curative properties of voodoo poison on the coronary system, Monkeyfur had the house to himself. I tailgated him and Ginny all the way there. Flashing my brights, screeching around the curves. Me honking and honking, the neighbors coming out bleary and upset. Monkeyfur waving sarcastically goodnight. The garage door sliding down.

*

Assuming that Goat wasn't already blitzed, and therefore indifferent to the general principle of time, I could make my delivery to the CPZ and get back to the pharmacy without arousing his suspicion. The only problem was my hands, which kept a completely skeletal grip on the steering wheel. Whether from the near-miss of Mrs. Bialetti's embrace or from Ginny's feral disgust, I couldn't yet face Goat and Michele.

Taco Freddy was me and Monkeyfur's regular post-delivery meal and second favorite hangout, after the In-N-Out off Arrow Highway. Across the street, you could rent industrial vehicles – caterpillars and cherry pickers and earthmovers. Next door stood an open-air market where a fake ID could score a case of Meisterbrau. Or, if you were Monkeyfur, something more expensive, like Corona.

Or, if you were Monkeyfur, you would actually be, at this moment, at Taco Freddy, playing Frogger.

Could he know already? Not unless Ginny told him, which seemed unlikely.

It was too late to turn around. I took a deep, deep breath and walked in, ordered *sesos* and a *horchata*, pulled a fifty-dollar bill from my pocket. This made me laugh; Mrs. Bialetti had been following me to my car so she could ask for her change.

I approached Monkeyfur. Despite my anxiousness, I couldn't help but admire his mastery of the Frogger machine. He didn't simply toggle the joystick. He used his head and hips, as if only the perfectly fluid, coordinated movement of his entire body allowed him to avoid extinction caused by serpents and alligators and cars.

He said excitedly: "I figured out the fly, the fly."

"You saw me in the reflection of the screen," I replied.

"Brilliant, Feinstein."

Feinstein wasn't my last name. It was a contraction for *fucking Einstein.*

"Painted on the urinals, urinals." According to Monkeyfur, it was *Official Linguistic Disturbance Week*. He was echolalic. "You know how they're always painted up and to the left of the drain? It's so you don't spatter yourself, spatter yourself."

There was always a pause after Monkeyfur spoke. Usually I felt like a cheetah keeping up with him. Cheetahs could run amazingly fast, but only for a short time, or else their brains overheated and they died.

"What are you up to?" I asked nonchalantly. I kept my hands in my pockets; my fingers must have held Ginny's smell.

"Waiting for you."

To clamp down on my terror, I imagined a Zen monk in a flowing black robe who, wanting me to recover my rapidly deteriorating calm, rapped me on the wrist with a bamboo switch.

"Exactly why are you waiting for me?" I said.

"Business proposition."

The fact that he didn't know didn't stop me from needing a minute to recompose myself. "Hang on," I said, "I have to piss."

"Don't forget to check out the fly." His Frogger gobbled some kind of bug. "And will you fetch my girlfriend? She's been in there forever."

"Are you kidding? I'm not going into the girls' bathroom."

The hallway to the bathroom was lined with posters for Negro Modelo Beer. Mexican women with bleach blonde hair, cleavaged black one-pieces. Sure enough, there was a fly in the urinal, though Monkeyfur neglected to mention that the fly had gotten itself caught in a spider web.

I let the lavender soap froth up in my palm. The walls between the bathrooms were as thin as a *shoji* screen, which allowed me to hear someone barfing.

What did Ginny just puke up? The very event of us?

With scalding water, I washed my face and hands. I scrubbed the skin around Ginny's address until it faded to a sunburn pink. Before the purple daisies disappeared, they turned into pinwheels and peacock's tails.

After I heard Ginny leave the bathroom, I counted out another minute.

In the tacqueria, a television mounted above an empty fish tank showed an image of a Texaco station. Ginny leaned on the Frogger machine, her hand in Monkeyfur's back pocket. It pissed me off. Though she had made herself up, she seemed drained, desiccated. Long, gaunt face with long eyelashes, and too much white powder on her face, as if covering up wrinkles from the future.

My food sat under a heat lamp. I put *pico de gallo* and marinated carrots into little plastic cups, found a seat far from Frogger, ate as fast as I could. The *sesos*, normally mushy and salty, had no taste. Each time Monkeyfur completed another level, Ginny french-kissed him.

"No tongue in public," I called. Why couldn't I shut up?

Ginny replied, "The only way you can get any tongue is if you order *lengua*."

"What were you doing in the bathroom?" I asked. "Expelling your imaginary bitch?"

"Don't call me a bitch, bitch." I could tell from her tight jaw that her tongue was flattening her gum against the roof of her mouth.

Monkeyfur didn't seem to sense anything unusual about the acidity of our banter. "I lost my guy," he lamented, "lost my guy."

They sat down across from me. Monkeyfur caught me gazing at the writing on the restaurant window - *sabado y domingo MENUDO!!!* – and asked: "Why would a boy band would name themselves after a soup? It's an insult to pig intestines."

I swigged down the chalky *horchata.*

"On to business," he said.

"Bad time," I said, my mouth half-full.

"As my wingman, I wanted to clue you in to my genius before we arrived at the pharmacy."

I couldn't deal. Abruptly I stood up. "Let's do whatever we're about to do some other day."

"According to Michele, Goat's beyond plastered," said

Monkeyfur. "Therefore today's a perfect day."

"Believe me, it's a terrible day. Don't come by." I walked out.

*

At my job interview, Goat pointed out wraparound sunglasses and depimpling ointments and those ring-binder paper reinforcements that tasted like paste when you licked them. He took me out front, where he deliberately dropped a penny. "Some kid's lucky day," he said. He threw another penny further down the sidewalk. "Generosity allows humans to live with themselves," he added. "And you need a healthy dose of generosity to work in this pharmacy."

"I like to help people," I replied. Goat nodded: the lame answer was the right answer. So what if my future boss was not only an alcoholic, as Monkeyfur had noted, but a walking fortune cookie? I imagined myself in Kyoto, writing *kanji*, learning the quiet, elegant art of bonsai, wearing an indigo kimono enlivened by a white-winged crane. Dad had called it prissy and refused to bankroll the student fee.

Soon I made my first visit to the CPZ. A malarial buzz spewed down from the fluorescent lights. It smelled stale and brown, like a petrified fart. In the hall sat a woman in a wheelchair. She was smoking; her hand trembled. An oxygen tube ran under her nose. The hem of her nightdress was soaked. Urine dripped onto the floor.

She rolled her wheelchair back and forth, blocking my path. I remembered how Goat told me to look everyone in the eye. Each person, regardless of physical or mental circumstance, had a fundamentally human need to be recognized by others. I remembered my vow to fight my abhorrence for old people, to treat every day as *keiro no hi*, or Respect for the Aged Day.

But the woman kept saying, "Hold me, young man, hold

me."

I pushed her wheelchair against the wall and scurried by, thinking: *there are degrees of human.*

That evening, I complained to Dad. "Suck it up," he said. "When you get old, you won't want some three-balled teenager treating you like dirt."

I didn't plan on getting old, I told Dad.

I called Monkeyfur. "They're freaks," I said. "I can't handle it."

"Get yourself baked, that's what I do."

"If you're stoned, how can you outrun them?"

"Come on," he said. "Do me this one favor." He needed me to timeshare with him. Paradoxically, his Dad would cut off his allowance if he didn't maintain regular employment. Plus how degrading, to work in a Mickey D's or Baskin Robbins; your scooper arm went mutant huge.

I kept the job.

*

What couldn't wait until Monkeyfur's next shift, and why did he need my help?

I had no doubt that Monkeyfur and Ginny would be waiting for me at the pharmacy. Regardless, I had bought myself some time. Maybe in fifteen minutes I might seem slightly less like an unfuckworthy impotent.

Probably Monkeyfur and Michele were skimming the register. It would be smart to do it during my shift; Goat would never suspect me.

At a crosswalk two blocks before the CPZ, I had to slam on my brakes for a woman with a stroller. I honked at her. Good chance there wasn't even a baby in there. More likely, it was a ferret, or a bag of potting soil.

I made the delivery, recklessly throwing the medications into a sink at the untended front desk (another dismissable offense), and drove back into the pharmacy lot. Against a parking stump stood a shopping cart. A bunch of wilted scallions hung limply over the child seat. Ginny stood by the pharmacy's back door, nervously smoking her menthols, two fingers callipered around the tendon of her elbow.

"Why are you even with him right now?" I asked.

"He called me. That's what boyfriends do, right? How could I say no?"

"You could act a bit more normal."

"I'm trying," she pleaded. "It's hard to fake everything being normal."

"Being fake seems easy for you," I said, flicking the cigarette out of her hand.

"Asshole," she said.

I went inside. Goat sat fatly on his stool, passed out, snoring. His arms splayed onto the counter. He must have been crushing his bulbous nose; no wonder he had sleep apnea.

Michele and Monkeyfur weren't stealing money from the register. What then? I heard them in the back office. To get by Goat, I turned myself sideways, sucked in my stomach. He smelled like hour-old puke and cheap whiskey – the kind used in Western movies to cauterize bullet wounds. Me and Monkeyfur would have to expand the GBS, or Goat Bender Scale, to cover this level of obliteration. This was at least a 12.

I saw Monkeyfur's hand digging into a jar of Ritalin. "You're doing drugs?" I asked.

"For teenagers," said Monkeyfur, "Ritalin is a gold mine. Grade-A speed."

"You've been letting Goat teach you about pharmaceuticals," I asked Michele, "to know what to sell?"

"It wasn't so he could get a woodie checking out my ass when I go up on the ladder."

When I got old, would some teenage girl show me her cleavage out of pity? Did Ginny pity me? To be pitied at sixteen, by a sixteen-year-old: what could be worse?

"Don't look all shocked," Michele said.

Goat let out a groan, settled back into his stupor. We didn't move. "Ask," the new Smiths single, played softly on the radio. Compared to anything on *The Queen is Dead,* it was weak.

The precise, thoughtful way Monkeyfur counted and divided the Ritalin made me think of Japanese gift-wrapping (*tsutsumi*), as if he would place each plastic baggie inside a balsa-wood box, covered in marbled paper or hand-dyed cloth, without wrinkle or visible Scotch tape.

"All you have to do is adjust the inventory records," he said. "For that, we'll give you – what did we say, Michele? Ten percent."

"About two hundred dollars a month."

"You're going to get caught," I said.

"We're not going to get caught," Monkeyfur said dismissively, "get caught."

"Can you shut up with that repeating shit?" asked Michele.

"Sorry, sorry."

"Then you're going to ruin Goat's business," I said.

"It's not my problem," said Monkeyfur, "if he diverts his

profits to his liver."

"You call him Goat too," said Michele. "Why go to bat for him now?"

I felt sorry for Goat, the way he made himself grimy and septic, the way he complained about the carapaces of crickets clogging up his storm drains, the way he bemoaned the fact that not one of his three children stayed on the west coast to help him ease into retirement.

"Pathetic and subhuman aren't the same thing," I said.

A sound like an unoiled swing came from Goat's stool. Somehow he had managed to verticalize himself, his body canted against the doorframe. Noticing Monkeyfur's hands full of pills, he slurred, "Stealers deserve to be incardinated."

Astonished, we watched him fumble for his keys, start lurching towards the front door.

"Fuck a duck," said Monkeyfur.

"Stay frosty," said Michele. "If he tries to fire us, we can have his license revoked. Monkeyfur, put back the drugs."

Michele hopped crutchlessly over to Goat. Softly she tried to talk him down. Monkeyfur emptied the pills back into their container. "Now that you've had time to consider," he asked me, "are you with us?"

I wanted to cut off his fingers.

Pretending to appreciate Goat's cabinet of oddities, the old-time pharmacist's rusty cylindrical weights and tin scales, I said: "Goat's trying to get us arrested, and you don't see any potential problems going ahead with everything?"

"I'm betting the bank on memory loss due to alcohol poisoning."

"You are so arrogant!" I could see him as a forty-year-old, a monogrammed North Hills High School class ring with an imitation emerald on his hairy knuckle. He would be a spectacular, transcendent waste, like that dead, 95,000-pound sperm whale that spontaneously exploded on an Oregon beach the year I was born, but still a waste.

"It's a lot of *unagi*, Mr. Miyagi."

"Screw your vision quest for the elusive F+," I said.

"Which means exactly what?"

At that moment, we heard a crashing of sticks in the hall near the back door, followed by a massive *whump!* As if someone punched a pillow. Michele shrieked. The seeing-eye sensor went off. And again, and again.

Goat was lying face-down on the linoleum. He must have tottered forward and tried to steady himself on the wicker basket full of rubber-tipped canes. The basket fell too, and the canes looked like giant spaghetti halfway out of the box.

Ginny hovered over him, one hand tugging at a crucifix earring I hadn't noticed before. She seemed concerned, though relatively unphased. I, on the other hand, started to see amoeba-like spots in front of my eyes, and I was sweating profusely. Previously, I had only seen unconscious people on *Emergency 51*. The blood on Goat's forehead and on the metal casing of the motion detector looked thicker, more opaque.

"Righteous!" yelled Monkeyfur. He held a cane over Goat's head, as if brandishing a spear. "Great caveman slay mastodon, mastodon!"

"Don't be a dick!" I said weakly.

"Just kidding."

"Besides," said Michele, "people remember shit."

"From the way his eyelids are fluttering," said Ginny, who

got 106% on her final Anatomy & Physiology test (answering extra credit on the Islets of Langerhans), "he's got a concussion."

Monkeyfur pointed the cane at my neck: "Dude, is that a hickie? Who'd you bang?"

That shook off my wooziness. "It's not a hickie," I declared, putting up my shirt collar. I made an effort not to look at Ginny. "Shouldn't we call the paramedics?"

"Help me roll this big boy over," said Michele, "before he suffocates."

We turned Goat onto his back. His breathing was regular. Michele pressed a Kleenex against the gash. "He'll survive," she said. "A couple of stitches are definitely in the cards." As she did any time the GBS hit seven, Michele went to call Mrs. Goat, who would arrive twenty minutes later in an Econoline van airbrushed with Florida's Okefenokee swamp. Sometimes she had to lower the wheelchair ramp to get Goat in.

"We should jam," Monkeyfur told Ginny.

He was right, as usual. If Goat regained consciousness and saw Monkeyfur, he'd remember everything.

But if Monkeyfur left, he would, for the billionth time, prove himself immune to consequences. I yelled: "You wanted to know about the hickie? Your girlfriend gave it to me."

"Sure she did." He sounded a little confused.

"I don't want to burst your bubble, but I did fuck her."

Ginny gave him a *no way in hell did I or would I do that* scowl.

"It's cool," he said to me. He had regained his confidence. "I get it. You're pissed about the drug scam, and about me being unkind to Goat."

It was a strange moment, like in a boxing video game where

the soon-to-be loser wobbled and wobbled, waiting to be knocked out by the victor's last brutal uppercut. All I had to do was insist once more on me and Ginny. Which I didn't do. Stuck in my head was this photo from the Kyoto program brochure: tens of people cleaning the subway stairs. With toothbrushes. It was an end-of-year purification ritual, a way of dividing the past from the future.

I looked at Monkeyfur, his permanently smug dimples and false, wide eyed contrition, and I concluded that this line between old and new didn't exist. I didn't want to totally clean the slate; I didn't want to totally destroy what the three of us shared.

"You're right," I said. "I was just yanking your chain. I'm sorry."

"No problem, compadre."

They started to walk out; I had gotten away with it. In a way, we had all gotten away with it. Until they reached the door, where Ginny started to sob and her hands and her gaunt cheeks trembled and Monkeyfur knew.

"Really?" he asked her.

She kept sadly, guiltily shaking her head.

Monkeyfur put his thumb and forefinger to his bushy brows. "It's true," he said, "you really fucked her."

I nodded. It was too late to deny anything.

He ran up to me and hurled me against the wall. His forearm pushed thick under my jaw, crushing my Adam's Apple. A minute ago, I was apologizing. Now the sudden, unexpected velocity of this pain made me spiteful, aggressive, and I managed to gasp out, "Fucked her." Mocking him.

Monkeyfur released me. My knees were jellied; I slumped down. He smacked a cane against the wall above my head. A white dust of drywall showered down on me. He grabbed Ginny's arm and half-dragged her out of the pharmacy.

"We didn't fuck," she cried. "Why did you say that?"

I sat on the floor until I heard Monkeyfur's Rabbit drive off. I stood up, got band-aids and hydrogen peroxide and cotton balls off the pharmacy shelves, and knelt beside Goat, who was snoring.

Michele came out from the office. "Impressive work," she said.

"I guess," I said. "Tell Goat I quit."

While Michele daubed a few spots of blood from one ear, I unstuck the Kleenex from Goat's wound, applied peroxide to his forehead. It must have stung; he didn't flinch.

"None of the band-aids are big enough," I told Michele. She shrugged.

I sort of hoped that Ginny was waiting for me outside; the biggest part of me felt relief that she had, in fact, gone with Monkeyfur. I screeched through the curves on Covina Valley Road. "Cities in Dust" came on; I cranked the volume. The video always made me nostalgic, the bubbling lava that flowed under Siouxsie's thigh-slit dress. Monkeyfur told me that it was about Pompeii – something about a *blanket of cinders*. Men preserved in antiquity by ash.

For dinner, I would make Ginny's specialty: corn tortillas topped with butter and sugar. She said the recipe came from El Salvador. And though I had almost finished my history essay on *Bushido* conceptions of honor, I decided to change my topic, to how the samurai integrated Confucianism into their codes. Dad would be so condescendingly pleased. I could see him cleaning out one thumbnail with the other thumbnail, calling me cocky for writing my assignments in pen. The bulk of your bright ideas, he often told me, will need to be erased.

II.

K/S

Dizzy peels back the shoulder of his angora sweater, revealing a red-purple patch of skin to RJ, who is sipping the last of his Coke from an Arby's cup. ---*Media's viral darling,* quips Dizzy, *in the flesh!* It's 1993. This year's signifiers: the lesion, a sand-haired boy begging research money from Congress. In the boy's suit pocket, a small plastic monkey; an anti-anxiety charm. Dizzy calls this first one his imaginary friend. No better evidence of bodily decomposition, ethical turpitude. Scored like a sewer grate, like a barbecue burn, open as a mouth. ---*I'm like so papular!* he says. Valley-girl style. RJ listens to himself sucking up air with a straw. Even a closed-mouth smile would humor Dizzy; to show shock would be to harden what need not calcify. Dizzy's been asymptomatic for a long time. The straw hits an ice cube and RJ thinks the word *calving* and Dizzy laughs though the joke has long since trailed away.

A few days later, with the first still in what Dizzy calls royal thrush, the second appears. Dizzy draws a five-pointed star around it. To prove his good health, he touches his toes, calls Sevil to schedule his weekly Turkish lesson. Once there, he makes her teach him nothing but spices. As RJ prepares for an "anti-date" with Misa – carefully guiding the razor around his short sideburns – Dizzy cuts bandaids into strips, applies them like jail bars to the sarcoma. ---*What are you doing?* asks RJ. ---*If one gets in your liver,* replies Dizzy, *it probably is colorless, don't you think?* ---*I think tomorrow I'll make us pancakes.* ---*Like you're coming home tonight.* ---*Of course I'm coming home.* That's RJ's plan, to stay close. ---*You're never coming home, you breeder,* says Dizzy. Watching Dizzy trace the lesion's scabby ridges, RJ says: ---*You know, we still have blueberries.* ---*Excuse me, I'm reviewing now. The word for thyme is* kekik. *Cardamon is* kakule. ---*We're lucky, it's so late in the season.* Dizzy yells: ---*Stop making everything all nice-nice!* RJ flops belly-down onto the bed. ---*Whatever,* he says. His fingernails need trimming.

---*I'll tell you a story,* RJ says the following evening, after Dizzy comes home, tipsy and self-satisfied, having seduced a boy with fragile wrists at a black-lit bar. Aside from a compulsory hug that morning, RJ and Dizzy have not spoken. What to say? Only that the world is big. ---*K/S,* begins RJ, *stands for Kirk/Spock. ---What about them? ---They're gay. ---Cool,* says Dizzy. The apartment smells of microwaved popcorn. While Dizzy gathers up the few remaining kernels from the blown-open bag, RJ describes the illegal underground novels that elaborate juicily upon Kirk and Spock's love affair. ---*Do you remember the one with the deadly flying amoebae?* asks Dizzy. *They look like my imaginary friends here.* He taps his shoulder. *And equally evil. ---Not evil,* says RJ. *Just misunderstood. ---Not evil? ---Until the end, Kirk and Spock couldn't figure out that they were starving.*

HOTEL GRAND ABYSS

1.

In the sequel, things get bloody. Suspense mutates to horror; body counts escalate. The start of *Halloween II* recaps the climax of *Halloween I*: Jamie Lee Curtis stabbing her brother Michael Myers with a knitting needle in the neck, wire hanger through the eye. Donald Pleasence, playing the psychiatrist Sam Loomis, shoots Michael six times. He falls backwards off the second story balcony, only for the camera to reveal the imprint of his body on the flattened grass.

Once it starts moving forward, the sequel allows us to witness the illusion of change over time. Despite the promise of closure, events rarely decloud. The neighbors, hearing gunshots, emerge from their suburban homes; terrycloth bathrobes, cordless phone. The father says: "It sounds like the death out here." Gravely, without a hint of kitsch, Loomis replies: "You don't know what death is."

The conclusion of the previous story: my father, desperate for his mother's whispery absolution, had forcibly removed me from her deathbed. I was furious (on my way out, I ripped a healthy leaf off the ficus in the foyer), but something in me had softened. My father was, for once, human, vulnerable. Despite his conviction that each of life's mysteries would, if discovered, submit to structuring principles, his heart still held. As grandma died, I sat in the back of Dad's car, my knees folded up against the passenger seat's magazine pocket. I popped honeyed peanuts, kept myself busy with a graduate seminar paper due the next week: why, in *Night of the Living Dead*, George Romero placed so much weight on the zombies' orgiastic consumption of the flesh they tore from the living.

At some point, I noticed that one of Dad's onyx cufflinks lay on the floor mat; probably he didn't know it had fallen. This resparked my resentment. I hated his mad professor routine. Even then, the man ran into doors.

Whatever benediction he received from my grandma didn't open him. To his credit, he didn't videotape grandma's funeral (as he had taped my twin brother's funeral). Otherwise, he made no further effort to close the gap between us. When I married Yukiko, our gift came right off the registry. He was skeptical, he said, of inter-species relationships. He sneezed at her relatives from Osaka without covering his nose.

As this sequel gets going, some fifteen years after the original, I am resetting the rubber seal inside my coffee maker, which this morning had leaked sizzling black drops onto the stove coils.

My father, I would guess, is sitting on the rollout couch in my sister Linci's home office, pouring reduced-fat milk out of his tennis shoe.

The behaviors we once called neurotic or flighty now alchemized into disease.

I take my Gaia Organic Blend coffee onto the front porch. I pick up a snail, set it on my palm. It moves a millimeter forward, then stops. It's dead, killed by the salt of my sweat. Wait: its slimy head just popped out. Thank goodness it's still alive.

I set it on the ground. Then I step on it.

In the sequel, I am an associate professor at UC Berkeley. Tenured. I am also, until this afternoon, the preeminent zombie specialist on the planet. The one who, at the café, substitutes the word "brains" for "beans" in photo-journalistic captions describing the coffee production process. "Once the brains are checked in and graded, they are spread by hand onto drying patios. The brains are baked periodically to ensure even and complete drying."

And my father? He's the man who, mealy-eyed, holds court with some form of invasive and irreversible dementia. He's the one in the Burger King, cutting open and emptying packets of mustard onto the tray while I order for him a Diet Fanta and a Whopper. Which he doesn't know to unwrap, and, once unwrapped, can't bring to his mouth.

2.

My sister Linci wasn't in the previous story – she was at Oberlin, studying comparative religion. It's part of being a replacement child, she says, to be written out of history.

Now she's stretching her hamstrings in front of a shop window (the scallop pattern of wiper marks, evidence of cleaning, visible on the glass) that displays antique wheelchairs with wicker seats. Linci always wears black lycra tights with either a gold or a silver stripe; today it's silver. I wear Dolphin shorts; a few years ago I found 20 unopened pairs at an estate sale. Candy-cane stripes, slit sides, mesh supporting fabric.

We turn onto Fulton. We run leisurely, a heart-opener before the hills. I am slightly wobbly, not having completely recovered from an inner-ear infection, and grateful that Linci isn't pushing the pace.

"So you taking him or not?" she asks.

On her twelfth birthday, Dad supplemented Linci's donation to Greenpeace by giving her a necklace of whale teeth. As a result, through her teens, she barely bothered with him. And for the last two weeks, while he, barely housebroken, has stayed with Linci and her girlfriend Shareen, Linci has considered him more as a lodger than a father, his stay temporary and non-negotiable. Either I take Dad to my house, she argued, or to the Rockridge Estates Convalescent Home (rated by Consumer Reports as the best in the East Bay).

"You know," she adds, "what he did yesterday?"

"He's not a freak show."

"He's not getting any less freaky. Can you parse that?"

I don't like how Linci runs, her floppy wrists and forearms; she says it conserves energy.

"He wants to stay with me," I say.

Which isn't true. It nauseates me to envision him in some glorified hospice, even if it has its own *Dance Dance Revolution* with rack-mounted defibrillator unit.

"That's sweet," says Linci, "but it's a martyr's proposition."

"Am I the only one who cares about him?"

"Don't be an asshole," she replies. "I love him. You don't like him, but you love him. The home will take care of him."

We pass the greenhouses where they harvest top-secret crops of genetically altered corn. "I'm going to keep him," I huff defiantly, "at least for now."

"Now is not an indeterminate time period. Now is ninety days."

Rockridge Estates operates on a quarter system. Every three months, there's an orientation for the new starlings, as they call them, allowing them to bond and imprint. And tomorrow morning is the deadline for their next intake group.

"You think he's normalizing," says Linci, "and bam! He throws his Cream of Wheat onto the floor. Take my advice, and do what Shareen's friend did when her cat started shitting everywhere. She put a Kleenex over each lump until it hardened."

"Disgusting," I say. We start to climb up Cedar Street. Linci tightens her pony tail. Quickly I'm too winded to talk, and I have to focus. The ground is fissured; the untrimmed rosemary bushes are giant afros that burst onto the sidewalk. Linci tells me about the preparations for tonight's party, a celebration of the release of her first novel. The title, *Hotel Grand Abyss*, is taken from Lukács. It's a mashup of the *Love Boat* and the *Inferno*. The protagonist is a woman known only as JM, who works as *Apocalypse Director* for the world's most posh and decadent hotel. In the first chapter, despite an ongoing spiritual crisis and pseudo-nymphomania, she has set up a flaming tar pit in the quarry below the hotel. Every hour, on the hour, a live goat is thrown in. Microphones amplify its death-bleats up to the guests.

I stop at the top of the hill. Hunched over, hands on knees.

"Bottom line," says a barely sweating Linci, "both of you will suffer horribly."

"Point taken," I say.

"But point received?" She starts to run again, which annoys me. At Memorial Stadium, girls are playing rugby. In the driveway of the hippie fraternity, an AMC Gremlin has a bumper sticker that says: "CTHULHU in 2008: Why Choose a Lesser Evil?"

Cthulhu, I recall, is a Lovecraftian demi-god of abject terror, unbearable to gaze upon.

"You're right," I say to Linci. She's surprised; she thinks I'm taking her advice. I smile, then add: "Point not received."

3.

As I rinse off from my run, I imagine how I will reconfigure my house. Install metal railings around the bed. Install metal railings in the shower.

I miss Yukiko. Even though Dad despised her on principle, she wasn't afraid of broken hips and ganglial cysts, she would have tipped his head to drink from spouted cups.

Purchase a cross-hatched gate so he doesn't fall down the stairs. Purchase no-slide socks in his favorite color, whatever that is. Knee pads?

I am childproofing my hotel.

As I pluck nostril hairs, (a laminated checklist taped to the bathroom mirror lists possible personal hygiene errors), I imagine how to reconfigure myself. Learn auto-hypnosis. Reduce the mysterious number of paper cuts I seem to pick up. Despite everything I've done to not be like my father, sometimes I can barely run the insinkerator without destroying a spoon.

Really: why do I want to take care of him? Maybe, as Linci said, it is masochism. Maybe I know I can't take care of him. I need to fail, which will compel him to talk about my failures so I can resent his resentment of the failures I've failed to avoid. Or I'm studying him. It's like having a zombie chained to a fence, limb by limb deteriorating off, to gather information about behavior under duress. What they tell us as they starve.

I brush out my shaggy hair. While Yukiko taught me to brush from the tips, to untangle the knots, I derive pleasure from the sound of the hair decoupling from my scalp.

Perhaps it's not a coincidence, me quitting zombies today. But why quit zombies at all? Here's why: this letter I received last week:

Dear Professor Dunkel,

I am a 2nd year PhD student in Popular Culture studies at Brown University. This year I am planning to apply for a Fulbright scholarship to Algeria – my mother is Irish, and so my EU passport allows me entrance. My project is as follows. I hope to write a high literary novel, a zombie novel, that takes place in Oran in 1948. Given your expertise, I would like to interview you on what a zombie state might look like at that historical moment, in a country on the verge of decolonization.

It would be, I hope, a worthy sequel to Camus' canonical novel The Plaque.

I love this letter. I framed it, put it right next to a napkin signed by Trent Reznor (*Dear John, thanks to you, I know how to survive a zombie attack in the tundra. Rock steady, NIN*). But the writer betrays his ambitions. Zombies, like other pop-culture phenomena, are mutable, easily assimilated. It's not that they lose their ideological weight, but their ideological time. For a while, we can use zombies to discuss more important topics; and then, when some South Korean company releases the first inflatable zombie sex dolls, their moment is gone.

"Why should anyone care about popular culture?" my father used to ask. "We're nothing but jellyfish swimming in the ocean of popular culture, we flow with its current."

We weren't discussing my profession; it was just another thing he tried not to understand.

I trim the triangle of hair on my chin, dress in denim, tighten up my turquoise bolo tie. My hair is still wet; I should dry it. No, they won't care at Oakland High, where in an hour I will give my final lecture on zombies, part of the "Professors Against Intellectual Poverty" campaign. The inner-city kids will ask the usual questions: if zombies are crackheads, if they sicken from radiation or virus, if they walk or run.

They, too, want to know why they should care.

More often than not, I tell them about a guy who, refusing to cry during his brother's funeral, developed a pus-filled cyst on his tear duct. Eventually the cyst exploded; the infection almost blinded him. The symbolic taking physical form. Zombies, I tell them, are that cyst.

4.

Laetitia, a sophomore, having sat on her hands fidgeting away the entire class period, her name printed cutely on a folded piece of paper, the classroom being a temporary trailer, a loud air conditioner blocking light from one of three windows, Laetitia asks, "Professor Dunkel, how come there aren't any freakin' black zombies?"

"Laetitia!" says the instructor, who gives me a worried look. She's some naïve twenty-two year old straight from Teach For America, paying for Xeroxes from her own salary.

But the question excites me. I tell the students that of course there were African-American zombies. "What about 'Thriller?'" I ask, to which four teens start moonwalking between the desks until the teacher yells them down. "What about the Sambo in *King of the Zombies? Night of the Living Dead*? African-Americans are absolutely integral to the zombie framework." I feel hum and sizzle over my skin, that rare moment when the ivory tower doesn't feel like an ivory tower. One of the other windows, made not of glass but of Hefty Bag, is sucking the breeze in and out, like an artificial lung the color of oil spill. "And why are there so many African-American zombies? Because zombie movies tie directly to the histories of black slavery. Blackness and death get yoked together, so to speak, and that's nothing but racism. While yes, the African-Americans in zombie movies do suggest slave revolt and social equality, most of the time, if you step back from the brains and blood spurts, all you can sense is the tremendous persistence of fear. That's fear of you, as oppressed, as outsider, as dangerous."

"That's obvious," someone says. "I want to know how come there aren't any black zombies from the hood. They all wear fancy clothes. Do all the black zombies live in Piedmont?"

Everyone laughs except for me and the instructor.

"Professor Dunkel is trying to teach you something important," she says.

"In a way," I mumble, "since zombies don't recognize economic boundaries, all zombies are from the hood."

The bell makes its merciful, detuned tremolo. Almost everyone pops up. Laetitia approaches my desk and gives me a fake lacquered nail, which she has ripped right off her thumb.

"This present," she announces, "is to remember that Class Nine schooled you."

The fake nail makes me unspeakably sad. My swan song, my curtain call: the only white girl in class, in the back row, her headphones on, deaf to the bell, who stuffs a piece of lime-green chalk up her nostril. And Laetitia with her friends, shuffling from the trailer, belting out a modified version of the Sister Sledge song: "We are black zombies, I got all my sisters and me."

5.

I'm walking on campus. It's windy, and warm for autumn. The branches of the trees that line Sproul Plaza are gnarled by leafless bulbs that resemble concrete-grey bee hives. I keep the fake nail in my pocket, turn it over and over, like a piece of lint, trying not to metaphorize Laetitia's literal pain into the lens of my own troubles.

Once, when I was studying for doctoral exams, Dad came to visit. We watched *Silence of the Lambs*. That night, he went on an absolute tirade about the killer's nipple rings. "Maybe you should write your dissertation on hermaphroditism and genital piercings," he said derisively.

"Transvestitism," I replied. I draped my arm around his shoulder. I couldn't blame him for his insensitivity, his anger, his melancholy (Mom, still asymptomatic in the original, had just died of ovarian cancer). He pined for something pre-lapsarian; parking meters that took nickels and dimes. Still, it devastated me, how unreachable he had become. How the next morning, breakfasting on my special bacon cheddar frittata, he insisted on catching an earlier flight home.

After I drove him to the airport, I let off steam in the basement of the Sproul Plaza arcade, repeatedly tilting a pinball machine called *The Machine*, which challenged you to assemble a perfectly proportioned female robot.

At multi-ball, she would purr, "Make me live!"

In part, my love for this particular pinball machine explains my failures with women; my goth girlfriend who would only have sex with me while wearing a black veil, and Yukiko, who spiked tea ceremonies with scotch, who at some point could no longer compensate for the fact that I played backgammon with myself. And cheated.

Now, as then, the white-boy protesters wear Intifada scarves wrapped about their dreadlocks. Out of politeness, I accept a flyer that proposes to jail Halliburton executives in the Iraqi jails they built. I'll use the flyer later, I have a new paper airplane design I want to test. I climb the marble stairs to my office, raise my computer from sleep, and open the following file:

To the Ever-Growing Legion of Zombie Admirers:

For the last twenty years, since my first book, "Zombie Renaissance: Divining Intestines in a Post-Capital Dystopia," I have mined – some would say invented – the field of zombie studies. Three years ago, the University of Chicago released my second book, "The Black Hunger: The Zombie Film and Critical Race Theory." My mission was not only to bring the zombie into the academic arena, but to bring the academic into the streets, to preside over zombie flash mobs and disaster preparedness exercises. And we have succeeded: the world now understands how central the zombie figures in our moment.

I may regret this decision; nonetheless, I feel that zombie studies must venture from their father. It is time for others to decode their discursive groans. Be assured that I am not turning away from the liminal in popular culture. It is (Woolf would not like such glib phraseology), a political decision as much as it is personal; the field between Lon Chaney and King Lear must be level(l)ed.

Respectfully, John Dunkel (kingZomB2@kierkegaard.berkeley.edu)

As I change the word "liminal" to "spectral," my cell phone rings. It's my father. He wants to play golf on Linci's Wii, but he can't figure out how to use the controller. Linci's in the office right next to him, but she won't answer his calls.

"I'm sorry," I say, thinking Linci selfish, "what about Shareen?"

"She's setting up the croquet pitch."

The balls, I'm sure, will be coated in pig's blood. The mallets will emit electric shocks.

I tell Dad that I'll teach him golf at the party. Afterwards, we'll take the Wii back home with us. Happily he replies that he wants to be Arnold Palmer.

I hang up, change "spectral" back to "liminal," cut and paste the file into an email, click the send button. At first, I feel the fresh-cut grass smell of new beginnings. My next topic of inquiry, the 1974 television series *Land of the Lost*, represents a perfect opportunity to explore the non-nuclear family, time portals and dinosaurs named Alice and opal-studded cave walls. But almost immediately, I feel stupid, paralyzed. No more invitations to lecture about the survival rate of deep-sea zombies at some Holiday Inn in Tulsa. No longer can I deduct fake eyeballs off my tax return. Zombies. Dumb staggering vegetables who don't shit, don't chew gum. I have no idea who I'll be without them.

6.

Towards the end of the party, my department chair (whose wife edited Linci's book) jerks me into my sister's study. "Zombies are your bread and butter!" he yells. "It's career suicide!"

Though he thinks zombie studies are for feminist psychoanalytics, he still makes me eulogize at all the faculty funerals because, quote, I have so much direct experience with death. At least now, he won't spend his time lurching towards me at faculty meetings, bulging out his bulgy eyes, his hands outstretched to give me my cup of chamomile tea. Trying to lighten his mood, I tell him about *Land of the Lost,* recite a fake OED etymology of the word Sleestak, wedged between *sleepy sickness,* a disease of pregnant ewes characterized by somnolence and neuromuscular disturbances, and *sleer,* verb, obsolete, to look askance. He frowns. Citing a phobia of scurvy, he goes scampering off for more mini-carrots.

I check on Dad, who stands in the middle of Linci's living room. As he takes practice swings with the Wii controller, he mentions quite lucidly that he'd like to check out the local pitch-and-putt courses. Then he asks about that round thing attached to the door.

"It's a doorknob," I say. I want to cry. I resolve to put up signs in my house that name each object, signs that display directions to other rooms, until the signs cover everything to which they refer.

Dad asks me if I want to play nine holes. I decline. I'm irate at Linci. I prepare, as evidence of her callousness, her refusal to convert her office into a bedroom for Dad, and her efficiency at the barbecue, basting each eyeless salmon with precisely four strokes of olive oil.

Outside, in the backyard, a colonial white model hotel hovers on the precipice of the empty swimming pool, which is covered in tin foil so as to look flaming.

I stomp up to Linci. "You have to help me take care of

him," I yell. "You have no choice!"

"Remember when we found someone's dead pet rabbit," she says, poking my shoulder with the spatula, "and Dad couldn't logically figure whether to put it into the trash can or the recycling bin?"

"What's that have to do with anything?"

Her friend approaches, and so I don't continue – I'll accost Linci later, in private. Sullenly I start scraping out the grill, picking at the black crust of charcoal and fish skin. They start chatting about the possible distribution of *Hotel Grand Abyss* to the Kindle. Someone inside the house lets out an anguished shout; it's Dad. We find him in the living room, staring at a quantity of blood dripping from his hand. With the Wii controller, he must have hit the Tiffany Lamp, which sent stained glass into his skin.

"Christ, Dad," says Linci, "don't move."

The golf game is replaying his last shot. At the dull, concussive thump of the ball burrowing into a sand trap, I know that I will give him up to the convalescent home. I know that never for a moment in his forgetting life will he forgive me. Avoiding the pieces of glass on the carpet, I take uneven steps towards my father; calmly I pry the controller from his hand.

MERMAID ANATOMY

That first night Lena brought us to the ship.

A ship that in 1860 ran aground keeling sideways on the mossy rocks.

Long before someone named this beach Ocean Beach.

Over time passing wave and storm buried the ship veiling it of what history it had.

Infrequent low tide years allowed the mast to breach its spindrift and very rarely as now could Benny and I enter through a gaping crack in the hull.

The ship unentombed unlike the cretaceously ambered bugs Lena wore on long chains around her neck.

When we arrived Lena and Benny and me hopped crab-legged off her scooter Lena explaining how the locals pillaged the manifest. Violating the Chinese girls on the wet sand letting the indentured slaves drown handcuffed in the hold.

Lena with the body of a boy kicked at the remains of a bonfire her skinny high-collared dress rippling like a red checkered tablecloth in the wind.

Her boot whispered everything to ash.

She blew on her fingertips saying to me *Flowers don't smell underwater.* Saying *And to think that four hundred years ago you owned the best part of this country.*

Meaning the Dutch bought New York for 20 US dollars siphoning it to the British for Surinam and an East Indies island silted with nutmeg.

We hoarded saffron dispersed salt huddling safe on our typhoid-scented marshes.

I vacationed in San Francisco friendless because c familiar path I knew as always shiny things with th qualities would seem equal and dull and crows with oily talons would sit overlording my eyelids.

Lena said *The object lies somewhere in the ship.*

Why don't you get it yourself?

I present you with the alternative of love or a garbage disposal unit and you choose the garbage disposal unit.

Her voice sounded like right angles.

Though soft like the felt that protects the corners of picture frames.

What does that mean? I asked.

It means don't choose the door hiding the Bolivian Llama said Benny.

Taking off his orchid-print shirt Benny with headphones blasting Don Ho said *It means just do it fuckface.* On his sallow back a tattoo of Godzilla and King Kong on the Empire State Building unaware how behind them faster than gravity Fay Wray was falling.

July blistered its *windkracht* bitter on the beach me having a memory of me at sixteen in panic interpreting my goose bumps as gonorrhea. Disease spreading an inflamed pink wave over my forearms. That summer in Italy with my grandparents my grandfather had apnea snoring as if meanly drunk me sleeping alone on a tarp under the trailer.

My *oma* each night before bed double-checking the emergency brake.

Lena sat cross-legged on the sand inside a dead campfire hanging a patinaed stopwatch letting it twist on its chain over a notebook me imagining Vulcan lonely and molten with his forge numbering the souls his labors would kill.

Having studied mythology the sideways lineage of deity and demi-deity I had no idea then how I had gotten the wrong god.

Benny might not recognize the object Lena said to me. *Only you can recognize the object.*

The maw in the ship's hull frightened me nightmaring fishless holes in blue ice. My so-called parents having died when I was seven skating a *sluis* swallowed down through the calving ice.

Apparently half-submerged near the hole was an upside-down Christmas tree.

And a laundry basket.

So I couldn't bear to look at the ship.

Blinking lights of offshore oil tankers anchored for the night bobbed and blanked out on kilometers of waves.

The clouds an occlusion of sky.

Next to a shattered piece of driftwood a doubloon found me. On closer look it was a gear-shaped game token from a place called Chuck E. Cheese.

Lena launched at me a paper airplane that veered nowhere near. *Get me the object* she said *I must touch the object.*

Her need absolute and compelling as the hum of electric wires on hackle nights when everyone save the sleepwalkers dreams shallow.

Remembering the hostel this morning when I first met Lena replacing in my hands my well-studied map with a map of Communist Prague. Saying *How tragic to find exactly what I expected to find.*

Let Lena be the map I told myself. As if from a riptide I

pulled back the storky ankles of my fear.

Straddling the prow on lookout for intruders cops or as he said *scuttlebags* Benny set his headphones on the deck. The strum of ukelele distorted against the warped old planks. He jumped through the broken hull and down helping my descent by grabbing my waist roughly or else blackly unbalanced I would have fallen.

The hull made timber-cracking noises reorganizing itself around us. It churned of rot and dead air you had to suck hard into your lungs and the moist wood smelled of every pocket knife incising initials on the rare available years.

The most efficient thing to do I said *is make a grid.*

Hey fuckface who crowned you Emperor?

In Holland instead of fuckface we said *kankerlul* which meant cancer dick.

If you stood on the Berkeley campus said Benny flicking at a lighter until it sparked *the girl moonies would swarm all over you.*

Don't cheat! yelled Lena.

It was an accident said Benny. The way his tongue curled down his lie made me taste how unrequited he loved her.

Light might help I said to Lena.

Psychogeography she replied *depends on experimentation by means of concrete interventions in urbanism. Think sailors snorting nutmeg across the equator think the filing of eyeteeth think firewalking. This applies equally to the gourd of flesh you call home.*

I lurched a step in the black hull seeing me not long after my parents died me walking down *Haarlemmerstraat* my eyes closed daring myself to walk one two three more steps blind to trust the universe not to shoot out a car crushing my pelvis each time too soon opening my eyes or now with my eyes open seeing nothing.

Why I enjoyed making love wearing earplugs.

Seriously I asked Lena *what's so important about this object?*

With one more question she warned I'd be reduced to buying sets of lacquered chopsticks my vacation doomed to febrility. Eating wrong-monthed shellfish on Fisherman's Wharf.

I'm going to etch a sketch now she said.

Grudgingly Benny agreed that so as not to unwittingly destroy the object we would inch our way crawling slowly in the claustrophobic dank from center to corners.

I wanted a *zeer oude Jenever* any antediluvial brown liquid that scalded down the throat.

My ears hurt from the whisk-whisk of Benny's hand sweeping the floor.

Ouch! he yelled *splinters!*

Benny are you okay?

Don't call me that fuckface.

Apparently his real name was James but Lena called him Benny in tribute to the recently deceased Rocky Aoki glorious spiritual leader of the Benihana restaurant chain.

Then why do you let her call you that? I asked.

You make a name sound like it contains every crust of you.

Our knees clomp-clomping the wood here in the hold with the ghosts of slaves.

I found something! I yelled. Something metallic shaped like a nutcracker.

Handing it up to Lena the distant halogen of the city explained me that it was severed from its cable a spring-loaded V-shaped clamp designed to charge car batteries.

I pulled myself up and Lena said *Not so fast* pressing hard into my forehead the ink tip of her pen *there's another object down there.*

What sense does it make I said *for you to hide objects for others to find to return to you?*

Lena walking back towards the water clapping happily her fingerless mint-green mittens.

The tetanus is coursing up my limbs said Benny. *If Lena set another object let's get to it.*

After five or fifty minutes of us trawling this second object Benny found what his hands felt was a bowl full of something crumbled. *Like a dog biscuit after the termites* he said.

Immediately I heaved myself up into the ocean air. Close by the ship stood a guy hunched over against the wind hoodie closed over his face and protective of Lena whom I didn't see I drove him off limping into the switchgrass.

Headlights in dotted spray through the dunes.

Benny held a ceramic dish with one fortune cookie in a bed of crushed fortune cookies.

Seemingly unburdened by the object cupping the intact fortune cookie in his two hands delicate as if a holy thumbnail-sized frog.

I asked where Lena was and Benny said *Those who know don't tell.*

So you don't know I said.

Willing Benny to open the fortune cookie because my *oma* who divined the future from bird scratchings in the gravel of bocce parks said man-made fortunes bestowed bad luck. He did read the fortune but was not as I anticipated immaculately fucked by lightning.

A Twix wrapper and tumbleweeds of crumpled paper dead in the ashes of campfire.

Crumpled paper had in my life always meant heartache.

I unwrinkled page after page on which inside diamond-shaped kites Lena had drawn a Mermaid with scaly grotesque flippers severed from the torso serrated in its unconjoining.

What's her story? I asked Benny. *She practically vibrates.*

As if I'm going to puncture her with language.

Fine let's share a taxi.

If we tried to hail a cab on Great Junction Highway at this time of night said Benny picking up his shirt and headphones *we'd be mistaken for male hustlers.*

I followed Benny at a two block distance curious about the stencil graffiti on each street corner of Galaxians who paternally ensured that the stencils of fluked whales didn't slip into the sewer draining into the bay.

Fog dissipating a hand's length over our heads.

Ascending the avenues and into Japantown where Benny closed an iron-barred door on me near an all-night Denny's where at 6:00 am I ate a Hawaiian grand slam breakfast with an ice-cream scooper half-sun of melting butter.

Licking the syrup off my fingers wondering what discolored planet Lena sprang from.

Lena who crumpled kites and broken mermaids and hid fortune cookies perhaps orchestrating some inarticulate salvation and in the glottal flap of her throat that stopped speech I recognized something of myself.

Overtipping a young waitress with bone-white dreadlocks whose nametag read *Velveeta.*

Then slotting in a quarter to fight Alzheimer's disease.

As Lena had insisted on wandering via algorithm generating *transient passage through varied ambiances* I started down Post Street resolving to enter the sixth open door which an hour after sunrise was an *Introduction to Aikido* class.

His foot stomping down the thick blue mat the sensei hooked his student under the neck nearly decapitating him. Never learning how to defend myself I watched raptly how unmovingly I sat not sounding the creaky metal chair.

Outside in the diffuse cold sun despite the pesticidal dew I lay down on a patch of grass.

Normally I slept twelve or fourteen hours a night but the mapless insomniac energy of Lena's west coast flooded me ecstatic emptying me well beyond the language of revelation and for some reason intensely scared of myself.

*

Just 20 hours ago I had arrived exhausted at the hostel where dropping my bags on the swept floor I heard the woman I now know as Lena explaining Benny that revolution was an improbable calculus of infinite subtle shifts in environmental atmospheres.

Frustrated she asked him *If you can't get that can you at least get me a peach smoothie?*

And a Twix.

Benny returned minutes later replying *They only have King Sized d'you still want it?*

Over her math-rimmed glasses Lena peered down at me saying *Only a homunculus could be fooled by questions of scale.*

Around her neck a silvery cricket made of smooth silken pebbles glued together like blobs of mercury.

2 am she said *Debord and Benny and I will be revving up for you.*

Later learning that Debord was the name of her scooter.

She left not waiting for Twix or smoothie which I drank after Benny with tennis shoes sparkly as disco balls looked everywhere for her and disappointedly left.

At first I forgot about Lena but after a day of block-legged dreariness at the Farmers' Market my cheeks wet from the juice of two-dollar pears watching pantomimes in Aztec plumage I as always critical of myself said *Doe je normaal asshole ben je gek genoeg.*

Act normal that's crazy enough.

So many years my friends and I followed script camping at Yellowstone hammering tent pegs with rocks purified by the vast Texan sky battered by hail on the Dakotan plains returning to Rijswijk wearing ten-gallon hats riding our bicycles through the needle-cold rain.

In my unsloughed tiredness I grew tired of our wildness cordoned.

And my *oma* who like puttying the holes in a smoker's tarry lung made me a *hagelslag* sandwich on a Delft plate before revealing that my dead parents were not even my real parents.

Adopted abandoned storyless to a bundle of reeds along the riverbank.

My childhood full of badly colored crumpled up connect-the-dots of giraffes and woodpeckers and *oma* showing me a waste bin full of paper balls enumerating the times she tried to tell me.

Though I imagined Lena in her brackish demeanor as a fake fireplace giving off no heat I had some want of her warmth her freckles as tiny hot coals in my hands.

At worst I told myself dressing at 1:45 am I would meet a different murder of crows.

*

Now arriving back at the hostel I expected Lena with scalene impulses waiting for me with battery clamp in mittened hand and explanation to part the beaded curtain of my half-consciousness but instead all the backpackers were blending their unique granola concoctions plotting against the ennui of their beatnik days.

Some people were driving to Mystery Spot where the laws of gravity didn't exist where billiard balls rolled uphill. One person inquiring for work received a generous offer from a made-to-order dildo boutique.

If dreams of molds of teeth meant the same thing as dreams of teeth.

How Lena's eyes gigantic and dilated as if blind until that moment taking the object from me through the cracked hull.

Remembering dimly that to save the mermaid from seafoam I must recognize her as the creature who saved me from the shipwreck.

Me dreaming me as her first vision.

All day I didn't brush my teeth or go to my room staying in the common area in awkward recline on the Thai silk couch watching for Lena.

The untethering weightlessness and wind of the kite ballasted by the mutilation of flippers. Scales of waxen wings melting freefall the inconsequent splash in the sunstruck sea.

Whatever this potential delivery into calm lit as a Christmas tree the brachii of my lungs. Everything glossy traveled quickly through air and each time I told myself I was happy I became a little more happy.

For eating a ham and butter sandwich with a knife and a fork other backpackers jokingly teased me which made me feel a part of something. Proud for exceeding the orbital pull of my quiet

I struck up a chat with the lambchopped smoothie maker who explained why gunfights in graveyards in Western movies were rarely conclusive.

Sadly by nightfall my mind started inuring itself to the flat reassembly of my initial plans.

The number 14 bus route to The Mission where I would eat a Nicaraguan breakfast of *frijoles negros crema y platanos.*

Waking up at 4:30 grinding my teeth horribly I had forgotten to put in my mouthguard.

Miserably unable to see Lena as the antidote to my eyes.

All these homeless symbols.

Two nights without her I proved myself taking different routes through the city. Based on the first letter of each ingredient in a Twix Bar correlative to Tenderloin street names. Counting the blinks of eyes I determined lefts and rights funneling up to a signless place locals called No Name Zushi where they sold fugu made from textured vegetable protein.

Hopefully removing the fake poison.

Even wearing neon orange earplugs my cochlea irradiated and dissolved again and again listening to a noise band made up of voice guitar drums and vacuum cleaner.

Reminding me of *oma* who as part of a radical socialist group stole all the fire extinguishers prior to tossing Molotovs into reactionary movie theaters. Who on days when I felt imprisoned by the imaginary hospital bars of my small bedroom cot would tap tap tap on my temples in morse code.

By candlelight drunk in the hostel a woman with a pierced cheek told me how last summer by moonlight she got paid to pick the slugs off the organic crops killing them into a bucket of salt water. Unable to implement such fluid genocide she dropped the living slugs at the property's edge thus keeping her in work since the slugs each night returned.

It would have been a *makkie* to mate with her but for fear of Lena's visitation.

Without Lena I grew increasingly weighted and lardish.

Nutter Butters glommed to the tongue tasting like wet clay.

The next two days I hardly left my room thinking of Dean Moriarty's boxcar binges and Allan Ginsberg's beard littered with pasta scraps and eraser shavings. Early the third morning I drank in dark bars with tight steep steps to basement bathrooms with saloon door stalls and whiskeys later in bright light I came out squinting to life itself finding myself in Japantown.

Sitting on a bench in front of Benny's front door unable to move I read the newspaper inking out another suicide off the Golden Gate Bridge where girls broken-backed by the fall relinquished themselves to the cold fast current swifting them out to sea.

Certain now that the mermaid in all her girlish desire represented some traumatic degraded time Lena's legs unlike the battery clamp unopened.

In order to truly desire a mermaid flippering green and kelpy you had to force yourself to forget she had no vagina.

Despondent I prayed for an earthquake to uncommit me through a crack in the floor.

The night before my flight I lost the hostel's corkscrew estimating if I broke the bottle how much cheap Chilean wine would I lose how much glass my stomach could grind down.

Sniffing my armpits acrid of iron I managed to sludge myself to the corner store. There I saw someone shoplift a mirror and nail polish remover and me envious of the waterfall of shame or any strong emotion in which the thief would later bathe.

When I returned Lena with her rust-colored hair was leaning one-thighed on a fire hydrant blowing the sweet exhale of a candy cigarette up into the descending sky.

*

Each time Debord the scooter hit a pothole Lena's wings of scapulae sharpened and I tightened my stomach so as not to lurch forwards concussing my head against her helmet. Between us on the rubber floorboards patterned with a Maori tattoo sat a purple-strapped duffelbag its logo of silvery winged shoes.

This immovable space between us like sixth graders slow dancing.

My fake mom riding me on the back of her *omafiets* touching my hand so I could hold tighter before crossing the tram tracks at the entrance to *Rembrandtpark*. Us plugging our noses passing the Renault garage.

At a red light I asked Lena *Did Benny give you the bowl of fortune cookies?*

Lena lifted her fiberglass facemask saying *I didn't leave any fortune cookies.*

A crescent of militia blackout under each eye.

The replicant Rutger Hauer who's Dutch said to the scientist who gave him sight *If only you could see what I've seen with your eyes.*

If mermaids saw color in abyss where the pressure can crush a combination safe.

You just went home without us? I asked.

Sorry I've lost my tongue.

Lena went through the light before it greened. A nursery that sold palm trees inside terracotta pots reminded me of Chinese warriors readying for battle in great lines through the great lonely weeds. Warriors the unburnt brown of the single gingerbread cookie *oma* rationed to me each day after school.

Scarcity and restraint declared sacred in Holland as a blank church wall.

The parking lot we pulled into jutted out over the bay renovated lofts to the left a road to the right a tall fence in front locking us from a small park. Broken glass bottles concreted into the top of the fence warding off pigeons unzippered lovers and saboteurs.

The peaceful gauze of the scooter's motor winding down allowed me to ask Lena *Is Benny meeting us?*

With her unhelmeting came the smell of salt as if sea water evaporated on her skin.

Silence is an elephant she said putting her finger over her lips.

Undoubtedly the entire area mounded from landfill.

Having upturned our country from loam we Dutch carried in our hearts a soft spot for building something out of nothing trenching mud from the underbelly of the sea.

What did it mean to have a soft spot in your heart?

Some said a glass of red wine first thing in the morning killed the worms in your heart.

Some said Amsterdam was founded at the coordinates of a dog's sick.

Unsurprisingly there stood a statue of a mermaid on a matte silver pedestal. Some replica of the original Little Mermaid which I saw in Copenhagen near a hippie commune converted from a military base. The mermaid in Copenhagen fronting the placid harbor the stunning white wind generators across the bay in Malmo like giant mixers slicing up the sky and Greenlandic

Eskimos slumming down the nearby housing projects.

Sure now that Lena's stories culminated here under the polyp eye of the mermaid.

Something queasily sexual on the slatted park bench or in the clawfoot bathtub used as a planter for white lilies and the mermaid with her serpentine hair covering each unsculpted nipple.

From the duffelbag Lena handed me a plastic pouch and the trident-pronged end of a long power cord. *The outlet's there* she said showing me the plug on the nearest loft *disable the camera first.*

I guess we're doing something illegal.

You know what's illegal? her voice unhoarse unscratchy unrolling a set of lock-picking tools from an oilcloth. *The blatant disruption of local psychogeography the unforgivable obstruction of the dérive the inhumane powers that satisfy oppression in a given environment.*

So we're doing something illegal I said drawing out lengths of cable.

Me glittering to accelerate for Lena some psychic aperture through the collision of fat sluggish molecules.

I resolved not to beg for past or future not to scavenge for her story.

Lena whispering into the hole of the lock.

On a brick ledge under the camera eye I saw that the plastic pouch Lena gave me was filled with a gum called BIG LEAGUE CHEW.

Pink with white powder burns compressed and helixed like orphan DNA.

A spoilered low-tinted Honda drove sudden down the street froze me lengthened me in light and I ground down my teeth.

Stretching I held the stem of the camera in one hand pushing the gum so it spread over the lens making us divinely invisible. Then wiping off my fingerprints removing the trace of me.

The cable plug entering the socket let through a lucky warm white spark.

Upon skipping back to Lena who had long since picked the lock who pointing ruefully said *It's so oppressively leaden here see how it gathers around her head?*

I tried to fathom a lead halo which didn't reveal itself.

Down the coast at the baseball stadium seagulls flew figure eights mini-eclipses fronting the banks of fluorescent lights. Me remembering one summer in Venice with *oma* and *opa* seagulls at night winging like this above a backlit colonnade. My grandfather charmingly failing to father me trying over pasta made black with squid ink to span the gaps of dark matter in my lineage said that as the seagulls mistook the bright light for daylight they never slept and driven crazy would die forever driven towards it.

It was the most beautiful thing I ever saw and the saddest thing I ever saw.

Lena had set a chainsaw on the moist soil strung out with violets and now drew a line of air from it to the mermaid's neck.

I picked it up let my fingers run over the saw teeth like a child's drawing of waves desperate for Lena to chip her story back into meaningless discrete chunks and yet uneasy craving its opposite.

Lena so far past her own powers she couldn't decapitate the mermaid herself requiring me as henchman as ritual sacrifice to the mermaid king who demands for his daughters men bloating face down in the sea or as ravager destroyer to lay waste to what?

I pulled the chain the blinding noise the wisp the pluming

smoke. Unable to gaze at the mermaid as I cut. Daggering chips of marble.

For Lena's ragged nails to stopper my ears.

Despite the shriek of noise in love with noise until the spark and grind of the saw momentarily stuck on the steel spinal column.

Finally the head plunked into the soil Lena let out a whoop again belying her tonguelessness. Making swimming motions with her arms parting the air as if its very consistency lightened before her and in her I saw the arrhythmic line of my lost days no longer lashed to me and the box of atrophy I had long secured around me in freefall like an open-walled construction elevator whose cable had been cut.

I took up the head indeed silver and heavy in my shuddering arms offering it up apotropaic to Lena positive she would throw the head into the water as humans having felt the mermaid's abjection must shunt her back to the sea.

If mermaids could return from land to conch underwater sounds beyond the frequency of human ears they would absolve our constraints.

Lena though looked pale and petrified. A charm of a praying mantis dangled the shadow of a scar in the hollow between her keybones. She started walking to her scooter and I ran after her lapsing into Dutch saying *Godverdomme* saying *Don't you want it?*

She put her hand hard against my chest me staggering backwards.

Jinx's palm! she yelled. *You must remain immobile!*

What happened to you here?

For the first and only time I saw her smile her crimped smile.

Don't look between the legs of women she said walking away *you'll turn to stone.*

Did she think I was imagining the shape of her body in her clothes nothing like the shape of her body?

Speeding the scooter almost flew into the water before Lena angled it away.

A light came on in a loft supposedly the artists there bred from recycled steel colossal articulated scorpions breathing fire into the cadmium night.

Walking home I hid the head under my shirt like a baby knowing I had gotten not simply the wrong god but the wrong mythology not mermaid but medusa.

Slitty harsh steel welts on my stomach.

So I retraced my steps back to the park stuffing the head into the duffel bag with its silvery wings slinging the bag over my shoulder.

Furthering myself from the water the mermaid's head grew shrunken and less meaningful.

From an all-night convenience store selling frozen goat cubes I bought for *oma* and *opa* candied almonds and keychains of Alcatraz.

Searching for change in my shirt pocket my hand haunted by the repulsing souvenir of Lena's repelling hand.

I left the mermaid in an alley where the still night air got small where I could hear every single cooling unit in the city condensing where pools of oily standing water shimmered but to my relief chose not my flickering phosphenic vision to reflect.

III.

FAILURE MECHANISM (VOICEBOX)

1.

Much Later

Kirby will push Trish down the stairs.

Bean will be walking down Telegraph. The Krishna Copy Center will amuse him, that a fringe religion where everyone dresses identically makes a living making copies. True, their food was stained the lovely, grainy orange of turmeric. He and Trish sometimes went there for two dollar meals on Sundays, though he never chanted, because he hated his voice, and gods, if any existed, couldn't be blue.

He will see Kirby in the Bongo Burger. The poser skull beads dangling from Kirby's sand-blonde dreads.

Everything will smell of lamb.

Kirby will say to Bean, "It was a mere mistake in anticipating distance, I swear."

The dull flecks of contrition in Kirby's drawl will not stop Bean from poking Kirby with an open safety pin he will pull off his leather jacket.

"If I see you ever again," Bean will say, "I am going to stab you. Repeatedly."

Tahini from Kirby's Persian Burger will drip onto the floor. "Dude," he will say, "lay off! Even Trish knew I was only trying to violate the air in front of her."

Kirby will sputter north, to a pot farm on the Lost Coast, without removing the pizza delivery sign rack-mounted to his car roof.

Bean will learn how to massage the sides, not the vertebrae, of Trish's neck. He will learn how to wait quietly for Trish to write out her requests, because Trish will not be able to form syllables. He will feed Trish more than 50 pounds of puréed spinach. Through blender, through strainer, through straw, through wired jaw.

Much Later

Under other circumstances, Bean would wrap his toes around the clover of the bathtub tap, let a drop of cold water fall, the drop warming through the bath water, transforming in descent, the tiniest of warm pulses atop his other big toe.

Tonight Bean will prefer, or deserve, darkness. He won't be able to see the shower curtain. The prints of squid, or octopi; he had never bothered to count the tentacles. He will stuff a towel under the door, to block out the candlelight from Trish's room. Why bother witnessing the naked self fogged into disappearance, degenerating in the mirror?

Slowly he will fumble for the lip of the tub. He will lower himself into the bath. The heat, almost unbearable. The nerveless spots, unable to differentiate extreme heat from extreme cold, so easily sunk into pain they knew nothing about.

Bean will lay there, legs akimbo, a butterfly angle that will pull slightly on the muscles. A small isthmus of water will run across him. If he lifts his hips, the water will drain, his groin will become dry land.

Once his father took him to an island off Washington State and there was land like that. A stretch of land like a bone spiked with beach glass.

And monks who made their own ice cream.

He will keep scratching at a stripe of hardened color on the tub, where his ex-girlfriend Cynthia had dyed her hair metallic red.

Atop the toilet once sat a bottle filled with Buffalo nickels. Cynthia had painted "I @ You" on the glass, apparently in menstrual blood.

Everything insensate, drained, or charged to negative. The skin, the bath, the area beyond the curtain, the three-bedroom apartment, all of North Oakland.

The body: aperture or potential aperture.

If he is truly seroconverting, the bacteria on the hair drain could kill him, and the cat litter, and maybe no more baths, and no more heat, and no more light.

Much Later

Bean will ride the Green Tortoise down to Santa Barbara. Sitting at the beach until one foot goes numb. Watching a vintage trailer regalia parade down Pacific Coast Highway.

The early model Airstreams. Silver, gleaming.

His mom will fight with the doctors about how much morphine his father could stand. She will ask Bean to stay with Dad in the hospital while she went home to shower. She will start dressing like an old century, starched denim tops and gingham skirts, dresses buttoned tight up the neck.

She will fall asleep, her forehead on the kitchen counter, knife in hand, making a peanut butter and jelly sandwich.

In the bay, after Dad's death: the strewn ash in the water and the bilge of the boat and the rot of stagnant kelp.

And the tiny broken crab carapaces that Bean will try to fit onto his fingertips.

Failure Mechanism (Straw)

A standard drinking straw is an outstanding delivery mechanism, simple and direct.

A bendy straw allows for wider vectors, at the cost of a structural febrility.

A curlicue straw maximizes delay. The potential for stoppages, for bottleneck.

A bottleneck, however, can be an opportunity, a release point.

Drink box straws have a sharp, painful bevel to pierce for the dark juice.

A straw can splinter, can be crimped, can be plugged.

The paper can dampen, become a spitball in its throat.

A syringe differs from a straw in how the body pushes or pulls the liquid.

An IV tube is a straw straight to the vein.

Any delivery mechanism suppresses multiple failure mechanisms.

2.

Lycanthropic

When Bean was a teenager, Dad woke him each Thanksgiving. Slanting forward over the bed, assuming the angle of a ski jumper, Dad said, "You're traveling through another dimension." He was a ringer for Rod Serling – the wavy brown hair and the way that, sitting in an armchair, he'd lean to one side, opposite from his cigarette.

"A dimension not only of sight and sound but of mind," Dad said, "a dimension not only of oatmeal, but of pancakes."

Bean stumbled downstairs in grey Gaucho sweats and an old mesh jersey. Mom handed a bowl of melted butter to Dad. Bean took the oblong pancakes to the couch, where he and Dad watched episode after episode of *The Twilight Zone.* Hysterical William Shatner at 20,000 feet, the electrical storm obscuring the lycanthropic monster scratching at the wires in the wing. Bean's favorite was the one where the banker dropped his pocket watch and time stopped and it was like he was the last man on earth.

Dad detested football. "If you want violence," he said, "you don't gussy it up in pads and Styrofoam."

Afraid of Asteroids

Each birthday, Bean's parents set an empty envelope on his bed. Bean researched worthy causes, like Greenpeace or Unicef, wrote his preferred charity on a scrap of paper, slipped the paper into the envelope, and sealed the envelope with a fake wax stamp that smelled like raspberries.

He never knew how much his parents gave on his behalf. Because he never saw the thank you letter, the tax-deduction form, or the subsequent queries for future contributions, he felt both generous and unrecognized.

Bean saved whales and rainforests and children with MS. He learned that others needed his help. He learned that baleen whales had four stomachs, and that we should be afraid of asteroids. No one on his baseball team cared, and in the dugout they kept chucking the ball into their mitts.

Grandpa Briny's Gift

Bean remembered his Grandpa Briny, Dad's Dad, as a guy who played ping-pong in the basement of his house in semi-rural Ohio. He told stories about swamp alligators. He sold security systems and Porta Potty-sized bank safes. Not infrequently, Dad told Bean, he came home from school to find the discrete components of some lock splayed out on the kitchen table. Briny, by no means a disciplinarian, foretold a gruesome demise to anyone who disturbed the spatial relationships of the exploded apparatus. More than once, Dad ate dinner while holding his plate a foot above the table.

"Ah," said Dad, "the contorted passings of the potato dish."

When Bean was nine, Grandpa Briny gave Bean a set of lock picking tools. On his tenth birthday, his father gave him his first lock, a simple pin tumbler. The locks Dad sent in subsequent years grew increasingly more complex.

The challenge: divine the lock's invisible mechanism with the touch and sound organs.

The rules: don't cheat, don't ask for help, don't destroy the lock.

Bean would sit in the backyard, directly under the tire attached to the rope swing, which he would set in motion as a pendulum above his head.

He would sit there until the click of the five pins lived in his ear.

And the spring's release of barely detectable pressures in the tendons of his wrist.

Even last year, Bean received a lock in the mail.

By then, Dad's bare legs looked like knobby sticks and his tan slacks hiked high and his black socks drooped and Bean didn't realize that it was Mom who had to write his address on the package.

No One Likes Hats

Mom had wanted to talk to Bean alone. She met him in the parking lot of La Super-Rica, his favorite Mexican restaurant. For the entire Green Tortoise ride, he had imagined the taste of a *chile pasilla*.

Unsuccessfully she tried to run her hands through Bean's long hair. "It's becoming a rat's nest," she said.

"I kind of like it."

"Your hair won't accept a hat," she said, "and your father was deaf, or recalcitrant. Which was it?"

Mom had always asked Dad to wear a hat when he played badminton, or went to the Farmers' Market, where each Saturday he withdrew 60 dollars from a standalone ATM and bought diamond-shaped soaps for the bathrooms and leafy vegetables that flapped around at the top of his burlap shopping bag. And after all that, Dad's skin cancer had crowbarred itself in through his bald head.

"Who in our family likes hats?" replied Bean.

"Can't you agree with me for once?"

"It'll get sorted out, right? It's like a giant mole?"

"Don't be naïve," she said. "It's in his lymph nodes now.

That makes it serious."

Supervolcanoes or Zombie Cockroaches

"Mom told me that you've known for some time," said Bean.

Dad and Bean sat on the unfinished deck, passing back and forth a glass of wine, which Dad wasn't supposed to drink. Dad had turned off the lights to better see the occasional stars, stars that disappeared when a patch of fog swept in. The twinkle of Lizard Mouth stretched open below them. It was October, and Bean wore black long johns under his ripped jeans.

"Things in the body come and go all the time," Dad said. "This one came and stayed."

"Why didn't you say anything?" Bean asked.

"They wouldn't have let me play softball anymore."

Besides, Dad said, it would have caused the gnashing of teeth, and by the time he became visibly ill, the world would long have been demolished by nuclear weapons or bacterial agents or supervolcanoes or Klansmen.

"Or zombie cockroaches," Bean added. When Grandpa Briny died, Bean had seen Dad irately crush a ping-pong ball against the table with his fist, so he interpreted Dad's soft-spokenness, his typically ludicrous humor as optimism based in scientific fact.

"Yeah," Dad said. "Or demonic reanimated Quarter Pounders."

Turbo Cart

Bean was a shift manager at the Berkeley Free Clinic, a half-submerged bunker near campus, where the homeless got themselves stitched up and co-eds got their STD tests. His salary allowed him to buy five-dollar Fugazi tickets, floretted yellow squash at Berkeley Bowl. In the break room, he argued with his colleagues about a project to retrofit shopping carts for homeless people, with reflectors and foldout tents and separation of recyclables.

"It will revolutionize American poverty," one man said.

"My cart better have turbo," said another.

"You think Scabway's going to donate carts?" asked Bean. "Give me a break."

By End of Year, Ash

"Do you think that in some weird way he was trying to protect you?" asked Cynthia.

As she tried to gauge how Bean was processing the news of his father's illness, Cynthia radiated a soft curiosity, the way one would touch a sea anemone.

Bean was lying on his bed, hurling a glop of silly putty at the ceiling, waiting for it to ooze, to fall. "Who gives – who gives a shit why he didn't say anything? Either way, he's probably ash before the end of the year."

Cynthia had never seen him so wound up; he could barely complete a sentence. She kissed Bean's forehead. That quieted him for a few minutes, until she once again heard the disheartening slap of the silly putty against the ceiling.

Skull Napkin

At the kitchen table, Callie studied for her MCATs. She could hear Bean and Cynthia softly moaning in the bedroom, sex sounds that mildly irritated her; they were someone else's sex sounds.

No more irritating, she thought, than a lawnmower before

noon.

The day after Bean got back from Santa Barbara, she had taken him shoplifting to replace his black sweater. At Buffalo Exchange, the in-house stereo piped in a flute version of "Love Will Tear Us Apart." Sucking her toothpick into her mouth, Callie watched Bean saunter by the cashier, who, studying for a Russian quiz, barely noticed.

Outside, two pre-teen girls were comparing butterfly tattoos, probably temporary, on their skinny upper arms.

"What do they know of Hopi Sun Dances or Bétamarribé scarring patterns?" asked Bean. His voice was an octave too high, whiny with irrational outrage. "Oh," he added, pointing down the street, "that must be their mom's Volvo coming to pick them up now."

The next morning, after Callie did Menstrual Extraction, and Cynthia was recovering from her late shift, Callie took him to Mama's Royal Café, where they both ordered tofu rancheros.

"Bean," she said.

"I know what you're thinking," said Bean. He didn't look up. He kept crayoning various skulls onto his napkin.

"Okay genius, what am I thinking?"

"My dad will be fine," he said.

Evil Moon

Bean met Callie in freshman year; she would say freshperson year. Drunkenly, she claimed that her magic power was the ability to sense the color of paint by smelling it. And he tested her, dorm room by dorm room, blindfolded. Snuggling in his single bed, they argued about whether the horns and stars on the Proctor and Gamble logo really hid Satanic symbols.

"No sirree," said Bean. "That's not a happy moon. That's an evil moon."

"It would crack me up if the family values company was secretly worshipping the pentagram. That they converted the board room once a month for the laryngeal possession, the raccoon sacrifice, the boneless limbo."

"How someone dances. The first time you see someone dance; now that is a revelation."

"Or someone's bookshelf," said Callie. "No one wants to see *The Fountainhead* on a cute person's night table."

"You should know that I don't dance. I mean, sometimes I jerk my elbows, like this."

"You have strong elbows, I'm sure. That might be your magic power."

"Once I moshed at a Camper Van Beethoven gig," he said. "I consider myself a promising mosher."

Then he kissed her, and their lips made a silly, overloud smack, which was the pixie spores of libido fireworking up and away.

Sewing Machine Versus Umbrella

When Bean seemed most paralyzed by his dad's illness, when he spent hours crudely chipping icicles from the freezer, Callie would start a game of Failure Mechanism. Originally she had called the game Sewing Machine Versus Umbrella, after the surrealists. Having recently caught the first Frida Kahlo exhibit in the Bay Area, she believed Kahlo's surrealism to subvert the patriarchal gaze over the female body. And so Sewing Machine Versus Umbrella became a fun, political game, something to tease out the unorthodox walkabouts of synaptic wiring, to pass time with juxtaposition, something for drunken nights when Callie's wonky

VCR spat out the billowed ribbon of classic movies.

"White rice and asbestos," Callie said.

Bean tilted up his chin; Callie could see his Adam's apple. "You mine both from the ground, and they once were supposed to be a good thing."

"Now they're sort of dangerous," Callie went on, "at the foundation of our houses or food chains. Lodged in our intestinal walls. We have to tear down everything we thought we once knew to get them out."

After Callie read Nicholson Baker's *The Mezzanine*, she changed the name of the game to Failure Mechanism. Any mechanism, she told Bean, contained the seeds of its own destruction. By locating points of overload and mistake, one could glean historical contexts, ideologically conspicuous absences, unspoken assumptions. A typewriter displayed its overwritings, could fail through mis-key, bad spelling, uneven pressure of the fingers. A closet held the promise that items in storage were meant to be hidden, secretive, opposed to visible display.

"When you build the first ship," Callie said, "you invent the first shipwreck."

"The body," Bean said, "being the first failure, right?"

"Take, for example, the flapping doors of the atria."

"I'd prefer not to," said Bean.

Bile Duct

Cynthia came in, quietly closing Bean's door behind her. Callie thought that she looked glum, or dissatisfied, as if Cynthia was the one in the kitchen stymied by the complexity of the bile duct - the Ampulla of Vater, the major and minor duodenal papilla.

The bile duct, they decided, looked like a thin-branched

tree in winter.

"The colors on that diagram remind me," Cynthia said, "of my first dog Shifter's asshole."

"Excuse me?"

Cynthia moved a fallen grape from atop the heating duct into Trish's compost jar. She told Callie about the plastic orange pumpkin in which she gathered each year's bounty, and how she would dump it all out on her parents' table, which was covered by a restaurant-vinyl tablecloth. "Once, Shifter ate a huge load of Smarties that had fallen onto the floor. I'm talking multiple packets here. You wouldn't believe the strange colors that streamed out of his backside!"

"Poor Shifter," said Callie.

"He was fine. And on that rainbow note," Cynthia said, pointing to Bean's door, "the darkroom beckons."

Private Pleasures

At first, Callie didn't like Cynthia. The henna-red tips on her brown hair made her seem girly, and she moved as if she was guiding herself consciously and precisely into a different mode of being. She walked with her hands splayed; braking, creating drag on the air. To Callie, Cynthia's blend of eccentric-stylish came off as affected, maybe calculated; the way she said "y'all" without ever having set foot in Texas, and she wore an overlarge belt buckle adorned with a swirling silver tornado, which just made no sense.

Sheepishly Bean told Callie that Cynthia was a stripper. So what if Cynthia's parents, first generation immigrants, owned a house in New Jersey? Cynthia wanted to make money grinding the pole, squeezing her tits. To individuate, or maybe to cover non-resident tuition, she kept a finger in her crotch. She worked the Private Pleasures booth.

Callie was by no means dogmatic about the myriad shapes of pleasure. She was, however, skeptical of its origins, which were, more often than not, governed by false consciousness. In addition to working at the free clinic and prepping for med school, Callie was teaching a DeCal class on female sexuality. She had read MacKinnon, had read Dworkin. Though she tried, she couldn't imagine an unmisogynistic, unobjectified world in which a woman stripped and danced for men, or for women even. Especially when women were making 60-something cents to a man's dollar.

Most anatomy books, she complained, located the clitoris behind the gallbladder.

It helped that Cynthia discussed stripping intelligently. "I think of it as a kinetic way to figure out something psychic," she said. Being around other women, especially at a pro-woman club like the Lusty, helped empower her, helped create women's community, helped shake off the cobwebs of patriarchy.

"20 bucks an hour, with a flexible schedule," Cynthia said. "Not bad!"

"I wish they were as flimsy as cobwebs," said Callie.

Panda Bear with Vampire Teeth

To cheer Bean up, Callie bought him a creepy panda bear with vampire teeth.

"Thanks," he said, tossing the panda bear onto his pillow. "I know you're trying."

Bean rode into the hills. He had a gorgeous racing bike, Bianchi's celeste blue, rumored to approximate the color of the Milan sky. He had painted it matte black, the theory being that a cheap-looking bike was less likely to be stolen.

Deliberately he kept himself in a too-low gear that strained his knees. He mashed the pedals. He didn't use his lights. He saw the cars coming down from Kensington, veering away at the moment they saw him. He smelled eucalyptus and fog and the salt from his sweat. He could hear planes dropping into Oakland, and water rushing into the drain, and the rustling of his jeans, and the Hayward faultline fissuring deep beneath him.

When he had exhausted himself, he descended, dangerously. He refused to tap his brakes, oscillating from black to headlight or streetlamp, skidding hard on some wet frond. The bike itself started shaking.

Forest of Pines

His mother asked him to come to Santa Barbara again.

"My cancer has refused to come to the negotiating table," Dad said. He kept talking with that endearing wit that made Bean want to punch the terrarium in the waiting room of the oncologist's office, where Bean read one of the Edward Abbey books that wasn't *The Monkey Wrench Gang.*

The oncologist spoke with a resigned, accepting tone. He sounded like dusty twilight in a forest of pines.

"Death's an equalizer," Dad told Bean, which made Bean think death was one of many sliders on a gigantic stereo, between bass and treble.

Lavender

The next week, Dad was sitting on a bench, watching Mom plant lavender. She bent awkwardly; the cartilage on one hip had worn away. Lavender, she told him, was part of the mint family, and could be used to treat wounds. "Oh," he said. Then he had a seizure.

The Lusty Lady

At 2:30AM, Bean drove across the Bay Bridge, arriving early because he didn't want Cynthia to have to stand around on Kearny after The Lusty Lady had closed. He sat at a 24-hour Carl's Jr., absently shuttling fries into his mouth.

How frivolous Bean's politics seemed! Recently he had put up a poster for an Anarchist gathering; now the gold-colored thumbtacks made it seem childish, as if he had sewed rhinestones onto his kaffiyeh.

If his father would never again look through his high-school yearbooks, why should Bean bother to wipe the sleep from his eyes?

Eventually he walked past the Italian restaurant, the one with clams the size of giant marbles, and waited outside the Lusty. The interior made him uneasy. A man Cynthia knew once paid her 100 dollars to masturbate in a kayak.

Afterwards, he bought her an ice cream from Cowboy Creamery.

And one guy he knew, a punk, would drive his girlfriend to turn tricks. He was so fucking emancipated, so proud of himself.

Cynthia came out. He told her he loved her, and that his dad was dying, maybe this week, and she asked if she should go to Santa Barbara with him.

"I'm fine," he said. "But I want you to do me one favor."

"Anything."

"Please don't go and fuck anyone when I'm gone. Okay?"

She was stunned; they had been monogamous for some time. "Of course," she said. "Of course."

Setting the Tempo

Callie saw Bean go into Trish's room, where Trish was sitting on her futon, testing the Gushing Spring acupressure point on the bottom of her foot. It upset Callie that Trish kept encouraging Bean to understand death as a passage. Not that Callie disagreed completely. Her timing sucked, that was all.

Bean gave Trish a quick hug and left for MacArthur BART.

It also upset Callie that Bean hadn't asked her, hadn't asked anyone to accompany him. He wouldn't even let Callie give him a ride to the airport. He was being selfish and narcissistic. He hadn't bothered to consider that she might want to say goodbye to his father, whom she had met on numerous occasions.

Still, because she played basketball in high school, she understood exactly why Bean went alone. Winning, according to Callie's coach, depended on setting the tempo. Full court press, a trapping 1-3-1, and a pass-first offense where the point guard pushed the ball up the floor. Heavy conditioning; wind sprints and shuttle runs. Callie played center. She was almost six feet tall, and had a smooth touch from the left elbow, and excelled at blocking the paint.

By setting the tempo, one kept an opponent off-balance. One could dictate terms, constructing the universe in such a way that forced everyone to accept its arbitrary rules.

Making everyone your dancing bear, she supposed, must help with coping.

Rodential Face

Ribbons of green bile, clumps of distended tissue. Dad's waxy, rodential face emerging from emergency surgery. The PACU: eighteen beds and a network analyst in hospital scrubs blithely running cables over the fluorescent lights.

Bean held his father's hand.

And Mom, purchasing a helium balloon in the gift shop and accidentally puncturing it in the elevator and her screams ripping open the air.

Failure Mechanism (House)

Bean's dad had a few days at most. It was nighttime, past visiting hours, and Mom had started a fire. "You doing okay?" she asked. She was leafing through a book on long-distance running.

"I'm not tired," said Bean, who stared numbly above the fireplace, at the original plans for the house.

The psyche is like a set of architectural drawings, he thought. Stuff is built on it. The physicality of the drawing itself, the blue pencil and eraser shavings. Paper and pencil are substances and metaphors turning into substances. Where the drawings are stored. How writing conventions evolve. All things get written on it, some get erased. Things get removed to make room for other things. Wires in the sublevels, the basements. Gas, heat, electric, water. The drawings written by many, approved by many, built by many. In the plans are mistakes and some of them are not fixed or even notated. The early drawings have dynamic lines and radiate possibility. Later it's a single line, calcified, meaning agreement or decision. Extras like wood and tile and sprinkler heads remain in storage. Sometimes the plans do not reflect adequate storage. The plans can be reverse engineered to understand the conflicting motives and dreams of the designers. The décor, too, can be reverse engineered. Light, space, elegance. Line, curve, elevation. How units of measurement change. How many cars in the garage. The tennis ball hanging from a string tied to the rafter. You can see corners cut where desire and feasibility cross. Always a point, always an X, where one grieves the impossibility of the ideal, tar-pit stuck between drawing and execution. Add-ons unreflected in the original plans. Eventually the house is demolished, shuttered, the land leached by memories.

Like drawing a cube and erasing the connecting lines between the two squares.

Sometimes you return to the plans and you do not recognize where you are standing.

The Shells of Flies

Dad died in the hospital. That wasn't at all the plan; he was supposed to come home for his last day or days. In his childhood bedroom, Bean waited for Dad's arrival, listening for Mom's car on the gravel driveway, pulling the desiccated shells of flies from the window moldings, as if completing a chore he had shirked years ago.

The Snow Cone Inside Him

"Did you talk to him yesterday?" asked Cynthia. "Was he cogent?"

"He said it felt like there were snow cones inside him," Bean said.

"Have you eaten?"

"I don't know. Maybe."

"Are you sure I shouldn't come down?"

"Don't bother. Besides, I don't even know the time frame."

Cynthia put Trish on the phone. "Breathe," she said. He liked that; it was obvious and achievable.

Callie said, "I'm so, so sorry."

"I wish we were at that Queer Nation protest," he said. At the Macy's on Market Street, he had roundhoused a mannequin of a dog wearing a white sweater with red snowflakes. Then they sprayed each other with perfume testers until their eyes stung.

Ventriloquist

Bean and Mom watched a variety show on TV. An escape artist, a ventriloquist, a pickpocket. The sync was off, and the sound of canned laughter didn't match when the audience opened their mouths.

Mom complained about how his dad hung clothes on the line, how he alternately overwatered and underwatered, how there was far too much money in the life insurance policy. Bean tugged on his earlobes and went out back. It was easier to climb the cinder blocks that protected the corded wood; he decided to climb the wobbly trellis. He sat on the roof, rocking precariously on the pitched shingles. He heard the whistle of trees, a cooing pigeon that should have been asleep.

Marathon

Mom didn't want his help with funeral arrangements. On the front lawn, Bean found a shriveled pumpkin from last year. Its skin had caved in, resembling a pale orange cow patty. The glass on the front door had a Christmas wreath.

Time itself seemed averse to or eager for decay.

Later, his mother told him that despite her hip, she was going to start training for a marathon.

The Shed

Because Dad and Bean picked locks so easily, they rarely used them, which made it odd that Dad had put a new lock on the shed.

"It's some fancy lock," said Mom, "and I can't find the key.

Can you open it?"

"You can't pay someone?" asked Bean.

"I'm not ready to pay any old schmoe to touch his stuff."

"Fine." On the way out to the shed, Bean made a triangle of a lavender stem and looked through it into the half-fogged sun. The silver bolt, he noticed, was the exact kind his father had sent him for his last birthday. Another oddity.

Bean ran to the garage for tools, ran back. His fingers were sweaty.

When he opened the door, he smelled the smell of hatcheted wood.

"Damn," he said. Everything, including at least one wall and a number of beams, pulverized. Not one unbroken vacuum tube, not one null indicator lying intact.

Dad liked to collect things to fix or reappropriate. Bean remembered how purposefully his Dad had stacked old wooden radios, or an old Atari 2600, which he joked about making into a planter for Mom, on the metal shelving units. A tambour clock, the kind that you put on the mantle. Sometimes Dad would choreograph strange tableaus; a plastic man playing bagpipes at the center of a model train set. Now the engines and cabooses and fake trees and general stores were wrecked, decoupled on the floor. The room smelled of olive oil that must have evaporated onto the concrete.

Bean couldn't tell if this was a deliberate spectacle, meant for others, or if it was a private, provisional destruction. Perhaps Dad was too weak to remove everything; the finality of that last seizure catching him by surprise.

Either way, Dad had been practicing the art of breaking down.

Bean plotted a course through the rubble. He looked for

a message, a survivor object. Immediately he lost his balance, had to lean on a fallen beam. He reached a table, which itself had lost a leg, and now held rolls of ripped-up gift wrap with a repeating pattern of leaping dolphins.

No axe, no hammer, no mallet. Why remove the implements of destruction?

Desperately Bean wanted to burn the shed, to keep the atrocity to himself. Once he had seen a photograph of Christmas trees, in France or Belgium, after the New Year. The villagers had piled the trees in a clearing. To celebrate or accelerate the passage of winter, a pyre would have to incinerate the dark.

Bean pulled an old toaster from beneath a bookcase. That, more than anything else, seemed earmarked for him alone. Why did Dad occasionally call him Toasterhead?

Then he realized that Mom stood in the doorway.

For some reason, he was embarrassed for his father.

"So that's what he was up to," she said. She turned around and left.

X-Ray Blanket

Mom wanted a traditional funeral. In his eulogy, Bean garbled something about pancakes being a delivery mechanism for maple syrup, and he listed all the syrups at IHOP, where Dad took him as a child, and he slapped the podium with his palm and some man's draped arm felt as heavy as an X-Ray blanket over his shoulder.

Impossible Laughter

Mom also wanted her husband strewn to wind and water; in the afternoon, they took his ashes to sea. Bean felt himself, not his father, delivered into something. A need to see everything vanished, undone. As the waves chopped onto the deck, he stood at the prow of the boat, refusing to hold onto the rail. He concentrated on those moments when he felt his heels or toes lift. Someone gave him some water with a lemon peel. He saw a harpoon mounted near the exhaust pipe; perhaps this boat had done some deep-sea fishing before renting itself out for cremations.

He wished he could grab the harpoon, shoot it up into the massing clouds.

He imagined the harpoon piercing the boat; the hole that its wake produced.

And the slow, tinkly rotation of a Ferris Wheel on the pier, and maybe laughter through the wind, which seemed impossible at this distance from shore.

3.

Much Later

The baby buggy, compacted and uncompacted so many times, will start to break down. Bean will oil the wheels, patch each hole with duct tape, write the date on the patch. He will ask for testimonials from the drug users he has helped, and he will keep them in a binder in the buggy, and he will thank each client "for fighting the fight."

Dave, who will organize the needle exchange's schedule and supplies, will give Bean a round loaf of pumpernickel from the organic bakery where he worked. He will somehow push a single candle into the top of the loaf, to celebrate NEED's one year anniversary.

"It's not only clients who feel grateful to you," Dave will say.

Thousands of clean syringes. Hundreds of lives.

Much Later

In the backyard of their new apartment, Trish will plant basil, an invasive spearmint, a Japanese maple tree. Trish will reconfigure her mouth to make different sounds. Though she will count the days until the wires and bands are unhitched from her jaw, she will admit that she has found solace in silence. Without so many words, her brain will fire less often, and she will feel more aware of her skin, more satisfied with the unlanguaged presence of others.

For Bean, she will make banana bread, using mushy bananas with big seeds.

She will read a book of Gary Snyder poems.

Bean will adjust her pillows on the couch, will turn on *Twin Peaks*, which they have recorded. They will have a VCR because Kirby, as restitution, will give it to Trish before going off-grid.

The opening sequence will come on; the laconic bass, the eerie green credits.

"Which character, you?" Trish will write.

"I want to be Leland," Bean will say.

"Not true."

"I'd love an alter-ego. Who would you be?" Trish will try to mouth something. Bean will hear "A-E-O-E."

"What?"

"Maybe Josie," she will write.

Puke Bucket

The Free Clinic was a drip in what Bean called the puke bucket. Triage, stopgap, referral point. Clients had their abscesses burst. Clients asked where to get clean and if methadone was replacing one addiction for another and if that disease really killed everyone fucking everyone and how long it took.

Bean said, "Best guess is nine ugly months. Take care of yourself, okay?"

"Sure," they said. Their tone expressed an awareness of some inevitable setback, the same way that Dave, a cautious man, talked about serious motorcycle accidents in terms of when, not in terms of if.

From Inside the Splash Zone

Cynthia's cat, Fruitloop, started making Cynthia's roommate allergic. Her fingers became mittens, and some prickly weed or dandelion gestated inside her throat.

At first, Bean opposed the idea of adopting Fruitloop. He didn't have experience with cats, had barely acknowledged Fruitloop at Cynthia's apartment. When Bean was a kid, the neighbor's cat would mewl for hours from the top of an elder tree. Bean remembered watching its owner use a long stick with an attached hook, a stick used to pull down high-hanging fruit, to prod the cat down.

"Cats are unpredictable and cruel," Bean said.

"Exactly," replied Trish. "Making them excellent teachers."

"I'll stay at your place even more," said Cynthia, "if that's okay."

Happily Bean cleared out his t-shirt drawer.

Fruitloop slept between their pillows, populated the carpet on the stairs with clots of hair. She let Bean play with her pads; he squeezed them so that her claws came out. And when he made Fruitloop jump and twist to catch a feather that he had stolen from the pet store, he felt a kind of all-encompassing glee that he likened to watching the orca from inside the splash zone.

Ceramic Bunnies

A month after the funeral, Bean started to attend ACT UP meetings at a church in downtown Oakland. The men he met wore tank tops or plaid silk shirts or biker jackets and some had sharp lines in their faces that looked like they were carved by floodwater and some took medications that made their skin overtanned, carotene. At times, a man would burst into tears, and at times, a man would push his hands out and say, "Don't hug me now, I simply can't." Bean listened to men talking about seeing other men one day and poof! not the next. A few men laughed at the word poof, stopped laughing. Men disappearing, as if America were Guatemala or Chile. Men who learned to hate, to fight legislated indifference, the varied species of benign and malignant neglect, blatant antipathy.

A kind of genocide, no other way to say it. Men talked about drugs that worked for a short period and drugs that didn't work and drugs that might work. Herbs, treatments, cocktails. Men who would do almost anything because they had to; because no one else would; because only outrage got anywhere; because silence, or patience, was literally death. Men sold their cars to pay doctor's bills and got fired from their jobs and died alone in the hospital because their boyfriend wasn't allowed to visit and the landlord throwing years of work, hundreds of ceramic bunny sculptures, into the dumpster.

In a World with Mukluks

Trish said, "Accept."

"Why? Why accept? Breathing, I can do. Accepting makes no sense."

Bean had lined all of Dad's locks chronologically along the back of his desk, which consisted of two sawhorses supporting a faded, sable-gray door.

Trish said, "What choice do you have?"

"The white gurus with plump white fingers who drive Bentleys and fuck fourteen year-olds, they also say accept. Men who make laws say accept, accept, accept."

Callie was making mussels; from his bedroom, Bean could smell the white wine. Laconically, Bean messed with Trish's hair, waist-long and wheat-blond, such a contrast to her squeaky, cheerleader voice, which didn't at all mesh with her job at a Himalayan imports store; flowing scarves and prayer wheels and lazuli rings.

In the kitchen, the boiling water had flown the pot. Bean had heard that sound once, on some trip to the Caribbean, fisherman dumping the day's catch onto the beach.

That thwap-thwapping on wet sand was the sound of death

and dying.

Dad had bought Bean a straw golfer's cap, a silver chain with a palm-tree charm.

"Good for them, those fish," said his father. "That's being animal, that fight. That's being honest about the violence of living."

Bean hated the martial vocabulary of illness. When someone said that someone fought their disease. How people bravely lost battles with cancer.

"I don't have to accept shit," Bean said to Trish. "And there's no God in a world with Nepalese mukluks."

Straight Man

At ACT UP meetings, Bean volunteered to work the telephone trees. He listened to men discuss hospital supplies and bedpans and walkers as if they were children's hand-me-downs. He wrapped stickers around the forks of his bike, staple-gunned posters of a bloodshot Reagan that said "AIDSGATE," offered himself up to be chained to the door of a municipal building, or the Bay Bridge. At protests, Bean handed out yellow flyers with treatment news from Seattle and pink flyers with corporate boycott info from San Francisco and blue flyers with legal counsel from New York.

Everyone loved him. They called him their straight man.

"I'm jealous of your girlfriend," said Dave, who had written his master's thesis on classical Greek sculpture, on the homoerotic fetishizing of hypermasculine knees.

"She's jealous of you," said Bean. "I wish I liked men, I really do. Those whiskers! Oompf. How do you deal?"

"I know, right?" said Dave.

Bean didn't know. Solidarity didn't seem to trickle down to the body.

After meetings, he'd ride past the Paramount Theater, past J&J's. Before heading into his apartment, he would go into the unused sauna, where he had once tried to grow tempeh. He would punch the punching bag that the landlord had hung until his sweat hit the dry coals and the coals did not steam and his knuckles felt eroded, as if containing small sacs of pebbles.

Anti-Vegas

Bean was flattered; Dave had asked him out for a drink. Bean locked his bike in front of the White Horse, rolled down his pants leg, wiped the sweat from his forearms.

They sat in front of the fireplace, which had real logs burning low.

"Easy to make," said Dave, referring to the gin and tonic he sipped through the mixing straw. "Just like me."

Bean laughed. He was fascinated by and incapable of promiscuity. "Do you have a boyfriend?" he asked.

"How do you know I fuck men?"

"Sorry."

"Seriously, is it my clothes? Be honest."

Dave wore his white, stretchy t-shirt, and made him look like "a baker's baker." When Dave was working towards his master's degree, he wore a white-collared shirt, as it, in his view, reflected the dress of Greek men. Both, Dave noted, made him look like a sailor up top.

"I guess I assumed," said Bean.

"Well of course I do, I was teasing. I'm a clear read. You, though, you're between everything. I would have picked you for fifty other causes before ACT UP, and yet you're here. Why?"

"That's a story." Whining about his dad's death would sound indulgent, so he told Dave about how he had treated HIV-positive people at the free clinic, mostly homeless and drug-using populations who had no voice at all.

"Do you think it's interesting," said Dave, "that you don't belong to one of the primary risk groups? You're not helping yourself, not directly."

Clearly Dave was testing him. "If we all treated HIV as fact rather than as taboo," Bean said, sticking to convictions he did truly believe, "we'd be so much further along."

"Yes," Dave said, "some groups get spanked much harder than others. You, for example, can pass. You can clean up your sartorial disasters and cut your dirty hair and fit right in."

"I don't clean up, do I? If I have to be honest, I'm here because ACT UP doesn't dick around. Isn't keeping people alive the greatest thing anyone can do?"

"Definitely. Nonetheless, I'm surprised that we haven't scared you away. If I can be equally frank, if I wasn't at this particular juncture of my life, I'd be sitting at home, making mint juleps and playing Nintendo. Totally apolitical."

"My parents raised me political," Bean said. "It's a matter of what kind."

"Not to mention learning about what you can't know, because of your emotions or your upbringing. It's all about what you do with yourself then."

The stereo changed from R&B to disco. Deee-Lite, judging by the vocalist.

"This music," Bean said. "So boppy."

"It's a carpe diem beat," said Dave. "Keeps you moving forwards. Relentlessly." He seemed almost wistful. "When you're at the bakery by 3AM every morning, you see things other people don't. It's quiet, and once a car drives by, everything has to restart from scratch, as if any movement at all stops the world from its necessary recovery. Like all the world's a version of Las Vegas. I'm anti-Vegas. Are you anti-Vegas?"

"I think so," said Bean. He finished his beer. "My parents took me there once. We got in late, and I remember my eyes hurting."

"That's right – too many megajoules of light." Dave stood up. "A second drink?"

"Sure," said Bean.

Despite its corrosive manufacture of spectacle, Bean actually loved Las Vegas. On that trip, his mom made a ton of money on a single blackjack hand, splitting aces. The bottom of the swimming pool was stippled with white cracks. He dived and dived, imagining himself a treasure hunter. There he found a penny, a blue casino chip, a pair of swim goggles with a broken strap. And to keep him occupied, his father taught him how to shuffle a deck of cards, how to make a bridge. When his parents went down to gamble, he ate a Cobb salad. Then he sat on the hotel room floor, picking up the unsuccessful riffles until he so proudly got it right.

All My Tattoos Are Literary

Cynthia was Sri Lankan; her parents spoke Sinhalese, taught her that death was a form of travel. Death wasn't something to accept, as she heard Trish say. Acceptance was something you had no choice about, unless you could raise the dead, so why bother forging a dichotomy between succumbing to and resisting a fact?

She was pleased that Bean came into the Lusty. He was chatting with the doorman, who had the word *Nevermore* tattooed over a Maori spiral.

"All my tattoos are literary," the doorman said.

Bean kissed Cynthia on the cheek. He looked as happy as he had in months, flushed and wild-eyed, which made her want to lie down next to him in Callie's car, like when they went on a camping trip in the Sequoias and had to wait out a storm in the back seat because they had forgotten the rainfly to the tent.

Bean let Cynthia drive Callie's car from the Lusty; driving helped her unwind. Bean told her how Dave had asked him to help start a needle exchange program.

"That's superb!" she said. "I'm proud of you." She wondered if fish slept at night, or if entire schools of them were, at this moment, swimming in the bay beneath her. She heard Bean clicking his tongue against the roof of his mouth. Playfully she put two fingers between his teeth to slow him down.

Special Order

"Sex is an everything mechanism," said Bean. It was 4AM. He was half-awake. "Light bulbs exploding in their shells."

"The sky sometimes turns blue-green," Cynthia said. "And flaky, like a catfish."

"A catfish?"

"Why not?"

He could feel Cynthia tugging lightly on his leg hairs. With two fingers, he grazed the vertebrae of her neck.

"Tell me one memory you have of your father," she said.

"Okay," he said. "Here's one. When we went to McDonalds, I'd special order my burger without the chopped onions. It infuriated Dad. He put his head down, pinched hard on the bridge of his nose. Even so, he let me have what I wanted. You ask because?"

"I like hearing you talk about him."

"As if I would eat that ammonia-filled shit now," Bean said.

"It doesn't seem like you talk about him that much."

"I do talk about him."

"True. I said you don't talk about him that much."

Bean heard Fruitloop scratching at the door. He let her in, picked her up, set her on the bed.

"Can we buy an iguana?" he asked. "That would be cooler than cool."

"Are you going to feed it live prey?"

"No sirree," he said to Fruitloop. "I would never let you get eaten."

Far Away Black Bear

Every time Bean had a memory of his dad, he realized that for some time he hadn't been thinking about his dad. He'd be sitting in his room, keeping busy, drawing the cover for a mix tape for Cynthia, and he'd be inking in the solid patches. His awareness was tight, confined: his wrist, his arm, the chewed pen. The paper, the line. Cynthia would be there, studying Keynes and the Stockholm school. He'd feel the mattress shift with her weight. She would read on her back, holding the book above her. That's how I work out my arms, she'd say, which made him laugh.

And then it felt like someone drilled a tiny hole in the window and a jet of freezing air came in and Bean remembered a trip to Yosemite, to Tuolumne Meadows, and a bunch of yellow flower parts that got caught in the rim of the spare tire in the trunk, which Dad asked him to clean out, and which he kept in a jar as a souvenir.

Or the climb to Half Dome, or the far away black bear they

spotted.

Which made him happy for the memory and utterly deficient in his grief. How many memories per day was enough?

Then someone put a tack in the hole, and again the air got stuffy.

His Labia

Bean had been stretching his earlobes, putting spacers in the holes, until they were almost an inch in diameter.

"Looks like my labia," Callie had said to him. Bean liked the idea of having labia on each side, like flanking bodyguards.

They were at the tattoo parlor. Between her left wrist and elbow, Callie had crooked lines of tattoos over each vein. Now, around her belly button, she was getting a tattoo of the Bread Basket from the Operation game.

The needle buzzed. He winced when she winced.

"It's not your pain," said Callie.

"I can feel it," said Bean.

Yes, Bean said to Callie, by doing the needle exchange, now named NEED – Needle Exchange Emergency Distribution – they could get fired from the clinic.

So what if he got arrested? It meant shit, compared to one life.

"Of course I'm in," she said.

They went over suitable locations, which had to be close to at-risk populations while minimizing the risk of harassment, surveillance, incarceration. Definitely not the Golden Triangle, a liberal white section of Berkeley, where residents pranced their Rhodesian Ridgebacks and dined at Chez Panisse, upstairs, to celebrate birthdays.

Callie said, "I don't get why you need me for the very first day."

"Who else is going to bail me out of jail?"

"Your girlfriend, or Trish."

"You know this kind of thing turns your pussy out."

"Hot, red-haired girls turn my pussy out. And you don't get to use that phrase."

"Why not? Do you own it? It's a free country."

"I'd slap you," she said, laughing, "if I could move."

They chose an area in West Berkeley, behind a cluster of Indian and Pakistani shops, a lower-middle class African-American neighborhood in an incipient phase of gentrification.

"That's where we'll do our dirty work," said Callie.

"Fuck yeah!" said Bean.

Afterwards, with Saran Wrap taped over Callie's belly, Bean treated her to Istanbul Express. They sipped double-boiled coffee. Bean even ate Callie's favorite, Turkish Delight, which felt like a great sacrifice, texturally speaking. Akin to eating jellyfish. He didn't care how rubbery it felt on his tongue.

Primly Clasped Hands

Cynthia drove; Bean put his window down. The series of dangerous merges onto the Bay Bridge exhilarated him, and he loved watching Cynthia flaunt the speed limit.

"My shift was uneventful," she said, "except I might have a stalker."

"A stalker? Show me what he looks like. I'll kick the shit

out of him."

"When I'm dancing, he doesn't do anything. He sits in the booth, his pants down, his hands clasped primly on his lap. He sits creepily straight."

"You mean erect."

"Yes."

"Have you seen him outside the Lusty?"

"Once. I don't think he was waiting for me exactly."

"I'll punch him in the throat."

"You think I can't handle him? You think a dark girl doesn't get undressed by men on a regular basis?"

"I think you won't punch him in the throat," Bean said.

They tunneled under Treasure Island, came back into moonlight. To Bean's left, the oil refineries in Richmond blew flames to the sky. He closed his eyes and listened for the mesmerizing whoosh each time they sped past a supporting beam.

Press Conference

At Cynthia's apartment, Cynthia put Mazzy Star on the record player, and Bean admitted that he hoped to get arrested at the first needle exchange.

"Why get arrested?" asked Cynthia.

"Because then we'll have a press conference, and the public will have a clearer idea of why we're doing what we're doing."

Gazing up at the ceiling tiles, Bean unveiled his vision of the press conference, which, he told Cynthia, would take place on the steps of the Oakland courthouse. "Here's what I would say: 'The distribution of clean syringes is not a moral issue. It is a health issue which Governor Pete Wilson refuses to address.' At that point,

I'd pull a syringe from my pocket. 'All we are doing is exchanging a clean syringe for a dirty syringe. Can a sterile syringe transmit Hepatitis C or the HIV virus? If you show a syringe on television, will teenagers locate the nearest drug dealer in the Yellow Pages and start shooting up? No and no. A clean needle keeps drug users from debilitating, fatal diseases. By punishing those who dare to help drug users, Pete Wilson is in effect saying that he wants drug users to die. Shame on you Pete Wilson!'"

"Nice," said Cynthia. "Maybe it's a little self-serving? Shouldn't it be a drug user, or some doctor who does the press conference?"

"A doctor probably won't, since they'd have more to lose by getting arrested. And no, it doesn't have to be me. It could be Callie, or Dave. Dave would be a great speaker."

Cynthia rolled on top of him. "I don't want you to get arrested," she said.

"It's not up to you," he said. "Or me. It's up to fate."

Baby Buggy

On the first day of needle exchange, Bean and Callie wrote the phone number of the pro bono lawyer on their wrists. Bean tugged a plaid baby buggy out from the trunk of Callie's car. On the seat of the baby buggy, Bean reverently set a two-gallon Sharps container.

"All hail the biohazard receptacle," he said.

The Sharps had a red handle and a white, in-petaled aperture that reminded Bean of a Venus Fly Trap; something seductive and soft, a mechanism without complexity.

"Baby buggy and Venus Fly Trap," he said.

"Not now," said Callie, who stuffed boxes of points and single servings of bleach and pamphlets for clean drug use into the buggy's undercarriage.

"Once inside," said Bean, "you either got stuck or had to keep climbing, stickily, inwards. A wheel could get stoppered, like a shopping cart. A rip in the fabric."

"Focus."

"I love this thing." He couldn't get his Doc Martins to undo the lock on the front wheel. Finally he forced the latch with his hand, but when he bent down, the dragging sleeve of his sweater attracted a sticky substance that smelled like a cherry Icee.

"Here we go," he said. "Bets on our first day?"

"16,000 needles," said Callie.

"I say 16. And I insist on pushing the buggy."

"Be my guest."

They started down Hearst, preferring to be mobile in order to prevent complaints from any particular homeowner. The Sharps container bounced around in the buggy.

"Someone needs a seat belt," said Callie.

They walked; Callie played with her toothpick. In his back pocket, Bean found a fortune cookie from Long Life Vegi House. He had meant to give it to Trish, who mingled their fortunes in a lacquered box.

He ate the cookie. Except for the name of the factory in Queens where it was produced, the fortune was blank.

Fifty minutes and no one came.

"Yesterday must have been the end of drugs," said Bean.

Twenty minutes more, then a man in an electric wheelchair doing a doughnut at the corner. The man motored towards them, braked suddenly, lurched forwards. His name was John. His head, weighed down by a reddish mop of hair, tilted to one side. He was wearing a Public Enemy shirt. His hands shook; he must have had some kind of palsy.

"You for real?" John tapped out on his Qwerty placemat.

"Sure we are," said Bean. His tone, as they had discussed with Dave, was upbeat, not too informal.

"I have dirty needles," John typed.

Callie looked in his side bag; the points were loose and uncapped, which went against every protocol they had drawn up. For safety, the client had to cap the points as well as place the points into the Sharps, and ideally the points would be rubber banded in groups of ten or twenty.

Bean lifted the bottom of John's bag, dumping the needles onto the typing pad.

"Bean!" said Callie.

"First client ever!" he replied. He took a broken branch and prodded the dirty needles forward from the typing pad onto the ground. He took the Sharps from the buggy and set it next to him. Then he kneeled, counting each needle as he carefully dropped it into the Sharps.

"Please give me twelve," Bean said to Callie.

Callie gave Bean the clean needles; he dropped them in the side bag.

"Have a good week!" said Bean. John typed out "thanks" and rolled back down the street.

"Jesus," said Callie. "Breaking rules on the first day?"

"You want to send him home?"

"Of course not. Next time tell him to bring a friend."

"Next time I will. We had to start somewhere, don't you think?"

"Yes," she said. "We did." She raised her hand for a high-five. Bean almost missed her hand entirely. As they walked on, she explained how to give perfect high-fives, which had to do with focusing on the other person's elbow.

"You have to look at something peripheral," she said. "Like at an eclipse."

The next high-five was loud, resonant; a man peeked out from a second-story window. And the baby buggy seemed lighter to Bean, more maneuverable, more lithe.

4.

Fistfuls of Cotton Balls

After a few months, after securing the support of almost everyone on the block, the needle exchange settled on a fixed location above San Pablo. Dave insisted on keeping the baby buggy, partially to hide the Sharps container and partially to remind staff about their symbolic baby.

"Like they would give one of those to me to adopt," he said. "I mean a baby."

Clients came to exchange their needles in Continentals and Cutlass Supremes. Missing side mirrors, rags in gas caps. Students came by bus, on skateboards covered in Mr. Zog's Sex Wax stickers, on unicycles painted like candy canes. A client jangled up, millions of long earrings, a moon-pale white woman with stringy yellow hair.

A client: never a junkie or a victim or a user.

"Be safe," Bean said.

He looked everyone in the eye; he made sure to smile. Sometimes his voice got raspy by the end of the shift.

It made no difference to Bean that not a single client came into money, as in a Dickens novel. People took stacks of pamphlets to burn for heat; people stole dirty points and got clean ones which they resold at inflationary rates to the people they had stolen from. At best, someone entered a better rehab program, or earned their GED, or moved across the bay, to sleepy Pacifica, to live with their tough-love yet sympathetic sister.

"You're standing tall for another day," Bean said. "That's not nothing, right?"

Dave brought boxes of day-old bagels and rye bread and when traffic was slow he tuned his motorcycle. "It actually purrs," he would say.

When it didn't run well, he would say, "Why can't I remove the grumbly?"

Callie said to clients, "I'm going to be straight with you," and Bean tried not to snicker.

"Popping dyke pills?" he asked. She had been spiking her hair.

"Check me out," she said, "skating up the Kinsey scale."

Once, teenagers smoking clove cigarettes took fistfuls of cotton balls to stuff up each other's noses. Callie wanted to chase them down. Dave was laughing, and so was Bean, whose shaking earlobes could now accommodate a small slice of lemon. "Let them go," Dave said. "Whosoever runneth away can't hurt us."

Parthenogenetic Shark

Cynthia had a tattoo of a parthenogenetic shark, a female that didn't require a male shark for reproduction. Bean loved how the tattoo wrapped itself over Cynthia's shoulder. He was tracing it for his next mix tape: King Crimson, Blue Oyster Cult, early Genesis. 70's power rock was, she claimed, one of a galaxy of black holes in her knowledge of pop culture.

"Kumquat," he said. "How can that name turn someone on?"

Cynthia, who was lying on the bed next to him, had taken the less extravagant Siri for her stage name. Siri was short for Sirima, ex-Prime Minister of Sri Lanka and the first female head of state on the planet.

"It can be funny and sexy at the same time," she said. Fruitloop slept between her legs, letting out almost sinister snores. "Don't make fun of them, they're my friends."

"Sorry."

Fruitloop stretched and arched and it pleased Bean when she settled against his side.

She had also caused one of his ink curves to go astray.

"Fuck," he said. "It's all fucked up!"

"Is it really so bad?"

"A minor apocalypse," he said dryly. He crumpled the drawing.

The Biggest Foam Mustache

Cynthia kissed Bean's forehead. "Now it's time to dye," she said, quoting *Blade Runner*, which they had recently seen at the UC. She had found it mildly patronizing, mostly on account of its pan-Asian vision of the floating world.

"Very funny," said Bean.

"I thought so too," she said.

She went into the bathroom, which Bean and Callie and Trish had painted a lovely persimmon. A poster of Josephine Baker, clothed, smiling at her pet cheetah, hung to one side of the medicine cabinet. The other side had a poster of Emma Goldman with her wire-rimmed glasses. "If I can't dance, I don't want to be part of your revolution," she said.

Cynthia dyed the tips of her hair red, put a plastic bag over her scalp.

"Can you hear me?" he asked.

From the bed, Bean started to loudly enumerate everything he should have done to enlarge NEED's scope. They had started far too late, shouldn't have waited for certain social and political agendas to fall into place, should have stolen the first syringes, done more outreach, and the scale was too small, and unnecessarily clandestine.

"Don't," she said. It sounded like an admonition, which she didn't want. "You're only one person."

She parted the bath curtain and stepped in. Bean's almost monomaniacal sense of purpose was new, since his father died, and she admired it. Unfortunately, his nagging series of what-ifs tapped into her own self-doubt. Was she equipped to accompany him through the shapes of his grief?

She had met Bean's father once, had liked him unequivocally. He was a skinny man who laughed a lot without opening his mouth, who argued vehemently for his love of rhubarb. In Santa Barbara, he had asked them to play softball, and afterwards they competed to fashion the biggest foam mustache with their root beer floats. For Bean, she kept the team jersey, The Whistlers, a red shirt with long white sleeves.

He didn't want it; he refused to believe that he might want a keepsake.

Was her frustration at his denials and displacements starting to show? She hoped not. But even her jokes weren't jokes. What if "time to dye" wasn't her just playing on a homonym? What if it was a semi-conscious reference? *Blade Runner* was, after all, a movie precisely about lost paternity, about not having a dad.

Waste

Having forgotten to put the half-filled Sharps back in the storage shed, Bean brought it home, where it sat against the wall in the living room, almost like a small, squat building in the shadow of Callie's ironically displayed basketball trophy. Around the trophy hung a necklace of rainbow-colored rings from last year's Pride parade.

Fruitloop sniffed at the Sharps, immediately lost interest.

Trish and Cynthia were sitting on the foldout couch. The bed no longer opened. Each time someone tried to fix it, one of the metal hinges chipped out an ever-growing dent in the hardwood floor.

"Your hair looks pretty," Trish said.

"Thanks. I might have accidentally stained the bathtub."

"No problem." Trish didn't want to ask Bean to move the Sharps, which Bean would take back next Thursday; the very sight of it made her sad. There was no recycling the blood, the dirty needles; who knew what toxic landfill they wound up in?

"You're a business major," Trish said to Cynthia. "Can't you figure out how to make us use everything?"

Trish reflected a great deal about how not to waste. She produced about a dresser-full of trash every month, if you meant her olive-green dresser, painted with periwinkle vines, that she had rescued off the curb. Despite the sign she had put up by the compost, Bean kept throwing his egg shells in the trash, which she then picked out.

"If it's profitable," said Cynthia, "companies will find ways to create less waste. But it's not going to save the world, you know. It's not like we can ship all the peanut butter stuck on the lid over to Cambodia. And it doesn't make any sense at all when you talk about makeup. Mascara, you can't transfer that; you'll get an eye infection. Concealer, too."

Trish felt chastised. Really, she always felt gawky around Cynthia. It was as if Cynthia was pointing out some graceful, fleet bird that Trish could never quite track. When she tried to engage Cynthia by asking her about her heritage, Cynthia, who had visited Colombo as a young child, gave curt answers.

"They do have Tom Cruise movies there," she had said.

"I have a confession," said Trish. "Sometimes I stick a

wooden coffee stirrer down into empty bottles to get out the last drops of lotion. Does that make me seem self-righteous?"

"It makes you a fanatic," said Cynthia, "not necessarily self-righteous."

So much left on the sea-floor of our food containers; sometimes it was more than Trish could stand. Or to see Bean shaking the Sharps container, so proud of all that waste, trying to guess how many needles rattled around in there, as if counting the innumerable jellybeans in the jar.

Jingo

In summer, when Berkeley emptied out, Bean overdressed. He'd mooch rubber bands from the free clinic to vice the soles of his boots to the toe. He'd wear ripped black jeans, because, although he tried, shorts made him look storky. The only Anarchists who looked good in shorts were the Spanish, the olive-skinned boys with the front and back of their hair dreadlocked and the sides shaved like a mohawk, straight from months underground in Ljubljana, a cultivated stripe of dirt under their nails.

When a regular client stopped coming, and Bean knew they were sick or in jail, or when they dealt H and then dropped off their points, or when the points weren't for them, weren't for them, weren't for them, Bean did get upset. Still, he was proud of himself for how quickly he regained his composure.

"That was an excellent interaction," he'd say to Callie if he had imparted a useful piece of information, or if he suspected that someone was inching towards a better path.

"Chalk it up," she'd say.

When a client named Jingo died, however, Bean couldn't shrug it off.

Jingo died at the Japanese Garden in Lake Merritt, and

Jingo's buddy had taken his needle, the one Jingo used to OD, and used it for himself, right there, five feet from dead Jingo, on the other end of the bench.

It stung Bean, this first client who had died on his watch. Agitated, Bean started rocking the buggy, and Dave had to walk Bean around the corner to calm him.

"You are here to serve the clients!" Dave said. Bean could tell how irritated he was by how he kept moving a black curl from over his eye. "We do not do this work for you to feel good about your life!"

"Fucking hell," said Bean, "we're useless. How do you cope?"

"Jingo is one person, Bean. We're doing long haul stuff."

"I'm serious. Can you answer my question?"

"You deal with it later, let it out somewhere else. Here, you maintain a sense of responsibility in the face of your individual trauma. Now can we get back to business?"

"Okay," said Bean. When the shift ended, he wrote Jingo's name in the binder, right next to the point count.

Red-Feathered Hat

Bean had bought Cynthia some fries and was sullenly feeding them to her as she drove home from the Lusty. He remembered, he told her, that Jingo wore droopy plaid pants without a belt and he had a faint southern accent and when he approached the buggy, he took off his red-feathered hat, because that's where he hid his points.

"I'm sorry," she said. "It's awful."

He stared out the window. She kept fiddling with the side mirror.

"He's coming in almost every night now," she said.

"Who?"

"You don't know who I'm talking about?"

"I guess I don't."

"Bean," she said, exasperated.

"Sorry." He fed her more fries, taking extra care to put a perfect line of mustard along each one.

Clinic Defense

That Saturday, Callie and Bean took their coffees and walked to clinic defense, where they taunted right-to-lifers, protected women coming in for abortions by forming human shields around them. There was one fundamentalist, an older guy, mostly bald, wearing gold rimmed spectacles and loafers, waggling a "Thou Shalt Not Kill" sign, whose voice hit a frequency that curdled waves of nausea in Bean's stomach.

"I've had it," Bean said to Callie. He knocked the guy's sign aside.

"Boo!" yelled Bean. Spit flew into the man's face.

The man backpedaled until he tripped on a curb, fell onto a patch of muddy grass that stained his rear.

"Arrest him! Arrest him!" he yelled.

"Give me a break," Callie said. She pulled Bean away.

"Don't touch me!" Bean yelled at Callie.

"Why bother with that jerk?" she asked.

"I don't know. It felt like he needed a fist."

Wolf Patch

Callie clomped up the stairs, holding the remaining half of an Uhuru Pie. Bean smiled, beckoned to her; she fed him a bite.

"Calmer?" she asked. "Because I need your veins for my Phlebotomist Wolf Patch."

The free clinic had an incentive system of stickers and patches: Stitch Removal Star, Head Wound & Bandaging Queen.

"You should have had my back," he said.

"I kept you from getting arrested, dear one. And probably from losing your job. Now will you help me out?"

"No," he said, "I won't. I don't want you rolling my veins."

"You do know that you're making your own life more difficult."

"I don't deny that." It was true; until she got her patch, he would have to do most of the draws at the clinic. "Fine," he said. He sat down at the kitchen table. It had curved chrome legs, like a violin, and one of its two leaves had a weak hinge. A few days after he got back from Dad's funeral, the hinge tricked out and sent his five-alarm chili plummeting, which he left spattered on the floor for someone else to wipe up.

Callie warmed the washcloth, applied it to Bean's arm.

"Am I supposed to not be upset when someone dies?" he asked.

She tied the tourniquet at his bicep, disinfected the area with an alcohol wipe. "We're talking about that guy Jingo? Oh my, he was sketchy."

"Should I be numb? Dave came down on me so, so hard."

"Can you even guess how many people Dave has seen die?"

"A lot."

"Friends, co-workers, lovers. How many well-meaning activists has he seen put their tail between their legs the first time things got dicey?"

"Probably a lot, too."

"Okay, here we go." Callie checked the bevel of the needle, sent it cleanly into the vein. She pushed the tube until she saw blood; no need to collect it.

"Nice," said Bean.

"You know why activists bail?" she asked. "Because they can. Dave can't."

"I get what you're saying. Either way, it was rough. One needs time to process."

She removed the tourniquet and the needle, taped a piece of gauze over the insertion point. "If it's really about Jingo, which I doubt, then do what you need to do. If it's about you, then get over it. As you know, keep pressure on that for a few minutes."

Trish was a fainter, so Callie went over to Cynthia's for more practice. Bean rode up the steep grade behind the Claremont, to the toy trains at Tilden. He drank water from a fountain, splashed more on his neck, which tended to turn pink when he sweated.

Someone was overfeeding the pigeons; an entire crop circle flapping by the pond.

Callie's logic, he thought, went like this: Jingo's death wounded him disproportionately because he wasn't over his dad. That made sense to him. What didn't make sense was the notion that he could use sheer force of will to obliterate the pain of Dad's death. He couldn't just be like, snap! I'm okay.

What he could do was direct his anger better. Dad, after all, had locked his destructive urges in the shed.

The Cloyne Party

One night, when Cynthia was cramming for a test, Trish cajoled Bean into going to a party at Cloyne Court, where Bean met her new boyfriend, an ex-Deadhead named Kirby.

"Dude," he said, "call me Kirbs."

Kirby was, in his words, "striving for stillness." To Bean, he seemed to vibrate; quavering fingers and tendons humming as electric wires in wind.

Mostly for Trish, who had endured a string of emotionally suspect affairs, but also because his talk with Callie had made him feel more hospitable, Bean wanted to like Kirby. He made an effort to bond with Kirby over the play-dead beauty of the house's overstimulated pet python. They shared a distaste for the dance floor strobe lights, which reminded Bean of the prizes he never won selling candy bars in grade school.

"The source of all light is in the eye," said Kirby, quoting Alan Watts.

To Bean's dismay, Kirby didn't give a shit about Apartheid. When Kirby was smoking a bowl, Bean saw him pull off his eyelashes and blow them into the wind, which seemed unforgivably wrong. It was a waste of wishes. And more than once, Bean watched Kirby hold a sizzling match barely an inch behind someone's hair, then look around to see if anyone was admiring his handiwork.

Bean wished he could lie down on a deck chair on the balcony and drink a few beers, or eavesdrop on the Cloyne managers, who were deep in discussion over how to plane a door. He didn't. He stayed in the common room, where he sat cross-legged in the near-dark, atop a picnic table pushed to the side, skeptically watching Trish clap in admiration of Kirby's *negativa.* Trish danced, twirled her flammable skirt. While Kirby kissed her, Bean ran through a list of friends and acquaintances, anyone who would teach him how to breathe fire, in case a situation arose where he needed to breathe fire.

Death at Cherry Level

Bean and Cynthia went into the city before Cynthia's afternoon shift. They had the last BART car to themselves, and Bean kneeled in front of her, between her legs. They joked about why strikebreakers were called scabs, why Felix the Cat was really so wonderful. The bag of tricks? The polkadot bowtie?

He seemed springier today, which was a relief. After Jingo's death, Cynthia had no idea what would open the Pandora's box in which he held his moods. It was part of the sine curve of grief, she figured, which operated like long wave cycles, or the altitude chart of a mountain range. Either way, his volatility exhausted her. "Meatbags," he had called any politician, forgetting that her favorite grandfather had once been the equivalent of a city councilman.

"Sometimes I don't know how to help you!" she had said.

Each time he dug into her, she felt herself depleted, and she didn't want to feel depleted, so she diverted them towards easy activities. They walked around Coit Tower. It was windy, so she pinned her hair back; his rat's nest was too bulky to be moved. He kept his finger in her belt loop. Passing a cotton candy vendor, Cynthia explained funnel cakes to him.

"They're universal," she said. "Even Sri Lankans have *jalebis.*"

"You know," said Bean, "I might feel happy today. Not mediocre, not middling. Straight up happy."

"Cultivate that feeling, you should."

At a bar in North Beach, they drank mimosas and played *Ms. Pacman*. Was it feminist? Better than being Mrs. Pacman, they agreed.

"Ouch!" said Bean. Blinky and Inky had converged on him in the tunnel. "Death at cherry level."

"That's gotta sting," she said. "Now it's my turn."

5.

Much Later

Bean will bike to the party supply store for 3D glasses and helium balloons and silly string. At the free clinic, he will hang streamers. He will make a mix tape of Trish's folk heroes. Trish won't smile because she still can't smile.

That Friday, she will leave for a month at Tassajara, to celebrate her open mouth.

Trish will hand Bean the pliers, sharp end down. Bean will pass the pliers over to Callie, who had the steadier hands.

Both Trish's friends and Bean's co-workers, including one who had anonymously left a baseball bat in his office, will watch Callie remove the wiring from Trish's jaw. Bean will hear the snip of the metal. Trish will flex the atrophied muscles of her mouth.

"Whoa," she will croak out. "My voice."

Oracular

In autumn, Bean underdressed himself, wearing his mangled black sweater, one sleeve cut all the way up to the elbow, which he wrapped around his wrist like a tourniquet.

At 5:59PM, Bean, Callie, and Dave watched John doing wheelchair doughnuts around the corner trash can.

"The Swiss precision of Drool Man," he said, lazily scanning nearby tree roots for spent condoms and orange needle caps.

"You mean John," said Dave.

"I don't mean anything mean by it," said Bean. "And I don't say it to his face."

"We are all disabled in more or less obvious ways," said Dave.

"Touché," said Callie.

Bean felt genuine affection towards John, despite the fact that he was not an easy client. He didn't like cops or crowds. He rarely followed protocol. He would knock his points onto the ground if anyone used the wrong tone in correcting him. And each week, Bean straightened John's coke bottle glasses, gently reprimanded him, cajoled him into making their lives safer and easier.

Today, someone had capped and banded the needles for John; 27mm, an unusual gauge, for his hard-to-hit veins. His friend graciously agreed to put the dirties in the Sharps. Bean set two boxes of clean needles in his saddlebags. A parking enforcement car drove by, and John didn't panic or get aggravated by its twirling light.

"I'm keeping my cool," John typed.

"That is what we like to see," Bean replied.

After John left, Bean joked about getting him a Ouija board for his wheelchair.

"Why do the disabled always have to be oracular?" said Callie.

"Not an oracle," said Bean. "A totem. As long as he's around, we'll be around."

Electricity Camp

When the first rush of clients passed, Bean found a trumpet-shaped flower for Cynthia. Callie got a bright yellow windbreaker from her car and handed it to Bean.

"Fucking charity," he grumbled, putting it on, fiddling with the sleeves.

"You forget your jacket every week." She skimmed her

fingers over her newly cut flat top. She was getting used to, as she said, the astroturf and prickliness of it all. "Now give me your headphones – I brought my stripper and solderer."

Three weeks ago, one ear went out. Bean couldn't tell if it was ear or eardrum. It disoriented him, not unpleasantly, to be half full of sound, half full of the day. Strips of tape didn't fix the problem, didn't reengage the wires.

"I like my broken things," he said. "Besides, they do work, sort of."

"You'd prefer them broken? Now give it."

"Wires are serious failure mechanisms."

"Splicing," said Callie, "prevents the failure mechanism by braiding two lengths of frayed or disconnected somethings."

As a pre-teen, Callie had gone to Electricity Camp near her home in North Carolina. Also learned at Electricity Camp, or what her friends called Camp Shock'emall: circuits, electromagnetic fields, and something called Franklin's Disgrace, which sounded to Bean like the name of a rollercoaster that made you lose your lunch.

Mystery Machine

Bean had never seen the man coming towards them. He walked with a penguined gait, knees slightly out, much like his dad during a jogging phase cut short due to underpronation.

Was Mom actually doing marathon training? He had barely spoken to her since the funeral. Once she made arrangements to visit; she cancelled when she learned that the hotel was hosting a regional Beauty Contest for 6-10 year olds.

As the man approached, he swung a Scooby Doo lunch pail. Bean could hear the rattling of the points inside, could see the stacked profiles of Shaggy and Daphne and Velma in the passenger's side window of the Mystery Machine.

Bean stood up. "Excuse me!" he said.

"Excuse me what? Are you suggesting that I comport myself in a certain manner?"

In Bean's experience, heroin users were mellow, accommodating. Sometimes, however, it was heroin mixed with PCP or speed, or the jitter of no smack, or the occasional speed freak.

"Slow down," said Dave. Callie came out from behind the baby buggy. Bean stepped in front of her.

"He said slow down!" said Bean.

First the man tried to pull open the lunch pail without undoing the latch. Next he flipped back the latch without opening the pail.

"Set the lunchbox on the table," Dave said calmly.

"You asked for it!" The man slammed the lunch pail down and swung his arm forward and the lunch pail flew open. The uncapped needles clattered into Bean and onto the pavement.

"Sorry sorry sorry." The guy wiped his free hand over his brow.

"Do you want us to block you from doing points?" Callie asked. "Then chill."

"No," said Dave. "Come back next week. You cannot engage in that behavior."

"I'm fine," said Bean. He tugged on his ripped sleeve. "Let him do his business."

The man exchanged his points, walked away, returned a minute later. "Here," he said to Bean, "take the lunch pail."

Bean shook his head. “Just go,” he said. “Just go.”

The man left. Callie said, “Dammit Bean, are you okay?”

“Nothing hit me.”

“It looked like they might have,” said Dave.

“They didn’t. I think one or two bounced off my sweater.”

“Why’d you get so close to him?” said Callie. “That was stupid.”

“I didn’t expect that,” Bean said.

Dave went to Everett’s for barbecue; he had fallen “head over hells bells” in love with the Beef Brisket and the Goop marinade. Only after Callie was helping another client did Bean surreptitiously check himself. One needle had flown right at his forearm. He didn’t think it had pierced anything, but it had. A tiny prick, a red dot, barely bleeding, where the point had broken the skin.

Failure Mechanism (Lunch Pail)

A lunch pail is a failure mechanism.

For bologna sandwiches and tapioca Snack Pack puddings that couldn’t be traded to some sucker on the playground of Peabody elementary school.

For the metal hinge that kept the lunch pail closed; its rusted spring.

For cradling the thermos.

For the free box at People’s Park, where someone had found the lunch pail and used it and discarded it behind the Andronico’s in North Berkeley.

The same Andronico’s where Bean stole Kalamata olives from the olive bar.

The same Andronico's where a man with a penguined walk found a lunch pail under a milk crate and decided it was the perfect size to hold his needles.

The warping of the metal box over rain and time and the cycles of heat and cold.

"Yeah," the man chattered to anyone, "Sonny and Cher were on Scooby Doo, I can attest to that much."

In autumn, the metal box opened too easily, and the dirty needle sparked the failure mechanism into overdrive.

Punk Soccer

Bean had played punk soccer a few times before he met Cynthia. No boundaries, no fouls, two backpacks to mark each goal. One Sunday, the soggy field smelled like bilge; an EBMUD truck was pumping clogged sewage out of the drain.

Bean went for a sliding tackle on some guy wearing a Ramones shirt.

"Hey Ho Let's Go" read the ribbon on the shirt, a ribbon caught in an eagle's beak.

Bean missed the ball, got the guy instead.

The moment the shift ended at the needle exchange, Bean started kicking hard at the legs of the literature table, and the buckling legs sounded to him like the grotesque sound of his sharp metal cleats snapping a human ankle.

Sea Lion with Food Poisoning

"Hop in," said Callie, who had packed all the supplies in Dave's van and was rushing to make a first date.

"No thanks," said Bean. "I'm going to have a beer at the

Albatross."

"You sure you're okay?"

"I want some free popcorn, that's all. Don't begrudge a boy his scavenging."

Bean had a Guinness before taking the bus to Alta Bates. He filled out the intake form, sat down. The familiar stink of hospital waiting rooms sickened him. Counting the number of noises made by a single vending machine. The insertion of each quarter, the acceptance and rejection of folded dollars, the push-button selection. The way the hidden soda can rolled through the machine. A man wearing a hair net was driving one of those motorized floor moppers. A poster, designed for last season, outlined summer food safety techniques.

In Santa Barbara, he had once taken an early morning jog with his dad. On the beach, they had come across a sea lion in obvious distress. The sea lion moaned, rolling back and forth on its belly. It was horrific; it made a group of little girls cry. Bean and Dad went to find a park ranger, who told them that the sea lion was okay. In fact, it was fairly common; a bloom of red algae had given the sea lion a case of food poisoning.

Bean went to the bathroom. On airplanes, he'd go to the lavatory to waste time. Bean knew better than to stare an eclipse – what about staring at a 100-watt bulb?

He looked at the light as long as he could stand.

Then he looked away, blinking out the pain.

Incredulous how something so inane and banal could kill him.

Indeterminate

Three hours later, they sent him home.

"What the fuck?" he said. "There's nothing else can you do?"

He knew there was nothing to be done. A nurse had cleaned and disinfected the wound. The chance of HIV was quite slim, the nurse said, emphasizing "quite." First, the points had to be infected and the infected blood had to be at the tip of the point, and still a living culture, and in a significant enough load.

If Bean was seroconverting, said the nurse, in two weeks he might have a fever.

Though stress would do the exact same thing.

"And you'll probably be stressed," said the nurse.

"I won't know if I'm dying?"

"Not for at least six months, or if you get really sick. Do you have the syringe? We could test the blood if you had the syringe."

"Would you want that kind of souvenir?" asked Bean.

New Toothbrush?

The bathwater clouded him, eclipsed external sound. Bean closed his eyes before going under. His nostrils remained above water, his head poised against the lip of the tub.

Underwater noise, an intermittent burbling of the drain.

At some point, he would be too weak to get out of the bath, to hold his head above the water line. Too weak to open the supply shed. He remembered making love to Cynthia until his arms were too weak to hold him, his stomach muscles flooded with lactic acid.

One of the needle's many failure mechanisms: it required a letting, a puncture.

A needle was never designed to be self-cleaning.

He was glad that Callie hadn't come home. That Trish didn't sleep lightly.

Dad let his fontanelle, the plates of converged bone, open again to the sun.

The disease did its work. Bone became ash.

His father declined slowly, before the seizure's vertiginous fall. Unlike Bean, who imagined for himself a longer, more terrifying curve, a gradual slide scarred by incidents and partial recoveries.

In the bath, he ran his finger over the puncture mark on his arm.

Any hole, even a pink speck of blood, could create any damage.

He thought about Dave. His giant grey eyes. The charming hole in his cheek where his scruffy black beard hair never grew. Who for years had returned indeterminate HIV tests, neither positive nor negative, almost certainly positive. Who would lie in bed for days, debating whether it was worth it to spend money on a new toothbrush.

6.

Wreckage, Your Totem Animal

With his headphones repaired, Bean cranked up darker passages of noise: Neurosis, GGFH, Swans. Chainsaw noise, sludgy noise. Grunge repulsed him; it treated anger like something you could hold in your hand, like a pet rock.

At the free clinic, he organized the supply closet. During his lunch break, he played pinball. He could barely feel his fingers on the flippers, could barely acknowledge the lucky thump sound of a match. Only when he bumped hard against the machine to deliberately tilt it did he feel anything, and that feeling was a bruising pain in his hip.

There was no reason to tell anyone about the needle stick. In six months, he'd either have a major life change or he wouldn't. What purpose was there in inventing futures?

He rode home from work. He climbed the stairs. He heard some music dweeb on KALX playing Brubeck. Fruitloop was lounging on the kitchen sill, and Callie was coring an apple.

"Yet another white guy jacking up jazz," he said.

"Brubeck slept on the floor," said Callie, "in complete solidarity with his African-American band, when hoteliers wouldn't give them a room."

"Fine. What I'm trying to say is that I prefer Michelle Shocked or some other lezzie shit." He went into his room, closed the door behind him.

"What's really going on with you?" yelled Callie. "You've been a crab for days."

"Nothing's going on."

"It doesn't feel like nothing. And I'm getting sick of it."

"Sick of what?"

"Boys who need hugs. Sometimes I think God's brand of narcissism is white boys. I'm telling you, Bean, don't let wreckage become your totem animal."

"Thanks for the pearl," he said.

He drowned out the Blue Rondo with *Filth*. Use your hands to build things, screamed Michael Gira. Use your hands to break things.

Delivery Truck

The next day, Bean told Cynthia he needed a quiet afternoon, maybe a nap, and was too tired to accompany her to Urban Ore, where she was hoping to grow her collection of abaci. When he got feisty, snapping something about getting tetanus in Urban Ore's junkyard, she wearily decided to let it slide.

Instead, he went to a pre-Columbus Day protest. He remembered an old commercial about a Native American man canoeing through the sewage river. The socialists lifted banners, waved around Bush effigies. *La gente unida, vencida!* In front of the Unit Two dorms, a miniature refrigerator, the kind rented by students, lay turtled on the sidewalk. Someone opened the door and pulled down their pants as if to shit inside it. He caught a colleague from the free clinic, a vegan, sneaking into the ice cream parlor.

A large Coke truck drove slowly down Haste. A Coke truck was an obvious delivery mechanism. The original formula had nothing to do with the current formula and so how could you use the same name for its liquid? Bean joined the crowd surrounding the truck. People were screaming insults, rocking it, trying to tip it over. The driver bailed, practically bolted down the street, which prompted a gutterpunk with a nose ring and flaming red hair and an MDC shirt and a baseball bat to jump onto the cab.

With his first swing, he spidered the windshield.

The liberals ignored him, chanting a rhyming couplet about peace.

Bean felt frighteningly awake. He felt like people must feel before being struck by lightning. He pulled his kaffiyeh over his nose and mouth and jumped on the hood and grabbed the Louisville Slugger from the gutterpunk and he smashed the windshield until the cracks extended all the way to the side and the glass caved in almost to the top of the steering wheel.

Exactly as he had planned his press conference, he raised his fist to the sky.

A phalanx of riot cops was coming, so Bean jumped off the truck and ran down Haste until he crossed Shattuck. He stopped under some shade. Panting, he took down his kaffiyeh; the hot, stuffy air got pleasant and cool.

Strangely, he felt no release, relief, extravagance. It shook him. The endorphins, the adrenaline had almost immediately dissipated. If anything, he felt a slow-moving sorrow, like watching a stream flow under a brittle layer of ice.

On the way back to his bike, he picked some rosemary. It had barely any smell, so he dropped it. Someone had stolen his back wheel, which, for the first time since his dad's death, made him cry.

Wriggling Worms

At NEED, he broke protocol, implored people to help themselves rather than to rely on public services. Recklessly he rattled around the Sharps container to settle the points. Not for the first time, he took the uncapped syringes straight from John's bag.

"Have we not already had this conversation?" asked Dave. "Leave your moods at home. If you can't do that for two hours, then don't bother coming."

"Are you threatening to fire me?" Bean asked.

"Get your head on," said Dave. "I've got no time for your diva."

Bean wanted to tell Dave that he had dreamt last night of being fucked by an infected man. Worms wriggling from the sores. That when he screamed no sound poured out. His voicebox mute, wrapped in a towel of wet lead.

When he screamed, what came out was blood, and a desperately flapping moth.

He also wanted to tell Dave he was sorry for the dream, which was wrong in so many ways.

"I'll snap my head on," said Bean. He tightened his belt. His sweater hung loose, and he wiped his sniffles on his sweater, and one eye was bloodshot. The sky felt like a trash compactor against his corneas.

The Ground Beneath Him

Two weeks had passed; he hadn't gotten anything close to a fever. Even so, he rarely forgot that he was probably or possibly dying. To excuse the string of days when he avoided Cynthia, he alluded to a new, incomprehensible sadness for his dad. Using his dad's death as a smokescreen made him feel even worse. As compensation, he washed Cynthia's clothes, bra bag and delicates included, saving her a trip to the all-night Washingtown on Adeline.

When he bought her a blank journal, the same off-red cover as his mom's checkbook, he couldn't help but recognize the gift as projection more than altruism.

Why didn't he tell her? It would be so easy.

It wouldn't be easy. When he opened his mouth, his knees would buckle. Boiling tar would coat the lining of his lungs. The ground beneath him was crack and hole.

Crash Worship

Because Callie was now officially seeing Jan, a well-known domestic abuse attorney who actually took notes with a portable tape recorder, Callie had been lagging on her MCAT studies, and ruefully decided to skip out on the Crash Worship show.

"Why are you pooping our party?" asked Bean.

"Cytoarchitectonics," she said. "Or, for the uninitiated, brain slices."

So Bean, Cynthia, Trish, and Kirby shrunk themselves into Kirby's old Corolla. From what Bean had heard, the orgy of Crash Worship, the goat skulls mounted on sticks, seemed shallow, overly art-school, the nihilism of ritual skimmed off its surface. Bean went only because he had reached an edge with Cynthia, a river Styx, his curmudgeon behavior crossing from unusual to unsustainable.

The car smelled of pepperoni. Annoyingly, Kirby kept trying to clean the windshield, which meant that wiper fluid sprayed around the open windows. The moon was low and large and almost amber on the horizon. Bean looked at his pinky, which twined with Cynthia's pinky. How long would he even have nerve endings?

They reached an underpass in West Oakland, below part of the freeway that had crumbled in the big earthquake. Not one square inch of concrete remained untagged. A hundred bodies danced in a mosh pit, fifty more writhing in a circle around them.

They got out of Kirby's car. The blasts from airhorns made them plug their ears, and the smell of butane overwhelmed their nostrils.

Something important was happening, a visceral force that Bean hadn't considered or couldn't imagine.

"You want in, don't you?" said Cynthia.

"I think so."

She frowned. "Then I guess I'll catch you in the intermezzo."

She squeezed his hand, went off to dance with some Lusty friends. Bean threw his sweater onto a traffic cone and leapt in. The drums were slow, dense, tribal. The walls of guitar hung and droned and fell, as if some monumental being held volume and intensity on a string. Caterwauling shrieks, distorted vocals. Bean thought he heard something about being pulled clear of muddy water. He hurtled towards the next figure, bounced off, circled around the pit.

Between songs, he panted, swayed. Someone gave him a cup of water, and he drank some, poured the rest on his head. He saw Cynthia, wearing a loose white t-shirt and tan mittens, because her hands and feet were always cold. She was dancing with one of her girls, which made him smile. He felt lucky.

The music began again. Two women came by, their white loincloths darkened with smoke, breathing fire in front of him. They were icebreakers, forcing people out of their way, demarcating the space. Bean had never paid attention to the sound of fire, the molecular explosion of fire and accelerant and air, which seemed to grant him reprieve from the stultifying world. The smoke made him cough; it felt good, felt like the body doing its job. As if things had piled up behind him and there was no way to offramp and coughing expelled the blockage. Air itself was a failure mechanism. For smell, for sound. Air permitted vision. The clarity, the lack of particulate.

Once one expelled air, there was a remainder down at the bottom of the lungs. An incomplete expenditure.

The exhale had to be total. You had to have nothing left.

It wasn't that he felt connected to a larger structure; it was an accounting of the cost of pretending he wasn't. In isolation, he used his loss to make himself unique. He needed the notion of a hero's epic journey because only something that vast could account for the span of his grief.

Instead, it made him crazy, belligerent, insufferable.

Now, he realized, he had to tell Cynthia about the needle stick, for no more grandiose reason than the fact that it had happened and was coursing through his brain chemistry and was part of his life.

Bean drove his shoulder into one guy, pushed from there onto someone else. He had lost nothing, or had no sense of loss, or had everything as part of the totality of loss. He felt himself one miniscule part of a pulsing cell, an organism that didn't know what form it would assume or on which frequency it would pulse. It was the smudge of smoke on his cheek, the way he steadied himself on another being, the second a cinder flared out at the ankle of his jeans, the swelling of his big toe.

Pain was the correct reaction to damage, the originary failure mechanism working its reactive magic.

He felt the spray of lighter fluid, which he smeared all across his face.

At the next break, Bean went looking for Cynthia, couldn't find her. He stumbled over to Kirby and Trish, anointed a drop of lighter fluid on Trish's third eye.

"I want to feel this way," he said, "as long as I live."

"It's kind of messy," said Trish. She didn't like it, didn't dislike it. Crash Worship was the opposite of the Indian Thali; a meal with parts that needed to be kept separate.

"It's unreal," Kirby said. "So much flame."

This made Bean remember the Cloyne Court party. "That's right," Bean said. "Kirbs here likes fire. I saw you with the matches, you know."

Kirby held a finger to his lips. "If there's no catastrophe, why be a narrator?"

"Sneaking up behind people is kind of cowardly." For emphasis, Bean poked him in the chest.

"Okay, Mr. Bad-ass, let's hit the pit, and we'll see who's cowardly."

"Pissing contest?" Trish said to Kirby. "Come on love, stay here with me."

Kirby and Bean joined the moshers. Two band members held flaming sparklers above their heads. Kirby slammed into Bean; Bean pushed him back. They laughed. For a second, Bean forgave him, since Kirby was also part of the organism.

Then someone undercut one of the fire breathers, the one with jangles on her suede boots. She breathed a jet of fire close to Kirby, who, avoiding the flame, tumbled out of the pit and into Trish. Bean saw one of Trish's knees turn awkwardly, disregarding the rules of tendon and bone.

It felt like a memory, he told Trish later, but wasn't, this scene that flared so briefly in his mind. He was watching the back of someone's head, someone who was spitting out toothpaste into a sink, which evoked this primal need in him to plunge that head down, to spatter the downrushing teeth of their open mouth onto the chrome faucet.

Bean saw the bowing of Trish's knee; he heard Trish scream; instinctively he jumped onto Kirby's back. He started punching Kirby in the ribs. Kirby elbowed one of his kidneys. Bean heard the drums stop. The singer, a bulky man, dropped into the pit to pull him away. Bean tumbled hard onto the concrete. He lay on his back, gasping, the breath knocked out, his forehead gashed, watching the dust of the collapsed freeway float around him.

Failure Mechanism (Amplifier)

"It was an accident!" yelled Cynthia, who had seen everything from her perch atop a broken column.

"I'm fine," Bean said. He sounded as if his vocal cords had gotten scratched. "Thanks for asking."

"Didn't you see him get pushed into her?"

"Even if it was an accident, he needs to be able to protect her."

"Bean, you can't save the damsel if there's no damsel to save!"

"He's dangerous. I don't like him with her."

"You told me that he's the most stable boyfriend Trish has had in forever!"

"Stable, my ass. Is she okay?"

"How should I know?" She let her gloved hands fall to her sides. "I'm tending to you! I'm always trying to tend to you!"

"I'm sorry," said Bean.

"I can't believe," she said, "that you're capable of this kind of violence."

"Don't be like that! I didn't start anything."

"Don't tell me how to be!"

As if to call attention to the fact that he, too, had been wounded, he probed the area around his kidney. "Until that moment," he said morosely, "everything was fine. I even realized something important."

"You had an epiphany? In this shitstorm? Wow. I do not want to hear about it."

They didn't speak. Bean saw Trish hobbling with Kirby

towards his car. The band started again. The amplifier sparked, gave static.

"An amplifier is a failure mechanism," Bean said, mostly to himself. "Broken knobs, broken vacuum tubes. Allowing for distortion and destruction and, within it, silence."

"What is wrong with you?" she asked. "Really: what is wrong with you?"

He didn't reply.

"Be that way. If you won't talk to me, I'm going to have one of my friends take me home."

Cynthia walked off. Bean sat there, watching people muddle around, hydrating. One man did a stage dive into a kiddie pool full of fake blood; a woman squirted chocolate sauce onto the crowd.

Distribution Center

Bean spent the night in the storage shed, where he slept under a table, using a bag of cotton balls for a pillow.

The next day, at home, he saw a pair of crutches and a roll of gauze, which could have been for either Trish or Kirby. Bean called a friend who had been planning to drive out to Stockton, where they monkey-wrenched a Safeway distribution center, spurting epoxy into all the locks. They were extra careful to watch out for security guards, mostly because Bean was too damaged to run.

His friend wore a tuxedo t-shirt and laughed at everything.

Safeway treated its workers barbarically. Their treatment of migrant labor in the grape fields and abattoirs was laughable. Even so, messing with the capitalist infrastructure that cultivated these inequities seemed to Bean so distant, so trivial, so devoid of urgency. All this infantile sabotage gave him no more than a braggart's drunken story.

He felt like a stingerless bee orbiting some boxer's head.

The trip did, however, give him an excuse. He didn't bother to pick Cynthia up at the Lusty. He didn't even tell his friend he was supposed to.

The Sadness of the Chrysalis

Cynthia sat in the Carl's Jr., her clothes in a bag, writing down the things she wanted to remember about Bean when, down the road, she was feeling bitter towards him.

Once they went on a date at the Stinking Rose.

Once they kissed for twenty minutes in the sociology section of City Lights.

Once with no moon they walked from North Beach to the water and it took too long.

Once they made each other fake noses with raw cookie dough.

They didn't care if raw cookie dough, eaten straight from the sausage-shaped package, gave you salmonella.

Didn't care how much toilet paper they stole from the Business Department office bathroom.

Once she let him win at air hockey in the basement of the student union.

Once Bean said he'd never ever board a boat again which made her feel like his new family.

Once he made her coconut curry with brown chilies from Sri Lanka which made her lips tingle.

Once they tripped in the redwoods and Bean lay arched on

a large rock and Cynthia had never seen so much iridescence pour out from a man.

Losing him was like having the cocoon in front of you without ever having seen a picture of a butterfly.

Without the butterfly there was only the sadness of the chrysalis.

Unreceding Wave

At 4AM, Callie picked up Cynthia from the Carl's Jr.

"I didn't know who else to call," said Cynthia. In the car, she massaged her calves; she had danced hard enough to make them sore.

"All this anger he has," she said, "it's not going to recede, not like a wave?"

"Probably not," said Callie. "Or not soon."

"And he barely registered that a man was following me. How terrifying that is for any woman, and how lame of Bean not to register it."

"You said *was*?"

"I had the bouncer unlock his cabin. He was so scared, his pants down, doing nothing. You know what I did? I asked him what his name was. The poor boy scurried off like a mouse."

Callie laughed. "I love your creep repellant tactics."

"Even with all Bean's been through, is it so wrong for me to need something back from him?"

"It's not wrong," said Callie.

Callie pulled up to Cynthia's apartment.

"I wish I didn't feel guilty for leaving him," Cynthia said.

She hugged Callie, got out of the car. Callie rolled down her window.

"I'm going to miss spending time at your place," Cynthia added.

"Me too," said Callie.

Cynthia walked past the garden plot that she had painted a bright purple. The tomato plants had already bloomed, had been eaten; now a bare line of conical wire frames rose from the dirt.

Before My Voice Goes To Sandpaper

The next day, Cynthia brought over cat food. She had never been to a pumpkin patch, so they drove the coast down to Santa Cruz. In Pescadero, where they stopped for a snack, Bean selfishly bought one tangerine for himself, one zucchini muffin, and didn't offer her a bite.

Cynthia felt an increasingly painful humming in the back bones of her head.

At the pumpkin patch, he sat on a bench, nursing an apple cider. Cynthia pretended to leap from one pumpkin to the next, as if jumping from stone to stone across a river, as if expending energy for both of them. She picked the two smallest and the two biggest pumpkins because she wanted her front porch to express size diversity. She paid for them and returned to the bench, where Bean was cutting cheese with a pocket knife.

"I can't do this any more," she said.

"I know."

She hadn't prepared anything besides her breakup line, so she didn't reply. He put a piece of cheese on a Triscuit and gave it to her.

"I've tried," she finally said. "I've really tried."

"I know," he repeated. "You should leave me now. Before you'll have to hold my hand and I'll piss the clear tube and the pores scab and my voice goes to sandpaper."

"What are you talking about?"

"I was going to tell you at Crash Worship." He told her about the needle stick and his remote, yet very real chances of contracting HIV, and how in the hospital he got fixated on the polish machine slurping up a Sugar Daddy wrapper.

"I'm sorry, I really am. That's terrible. But are you asking for my sympathy? Do you want us to stay together?"

"No," he said. "I'm not a good person any more. I'm not good for you."

"Then why are you telling me now? You had weeks to tell me and you didn't!"

"Like I said, I had been wanting to tell you."

"It's too much," Cynthia said. "How can I forgive everything that's happened?"

Bean started crying. She didn't console him. They watched patches of fog sift through the trees bordering the pumpkin patch.

"I don't know how to do what I'm supposed to do," he said. "I don't even know what I'm supposed to do."

"That's what breaks my heart," she said. "That's exactly why I can't any more."

A squirrel hopped up on the picnic table. Bean flung a Triscuit at it. He missed. The squirrel hopped off to find its new food.

Ocean of Storms

Callie had more or less moved in with Jan. She had postponed taking her MCATs to join the Lesbian Avengers, and was currently in Montana, learning how to breathe fire.

After Crash Worship, Trish barely spoke to Bean. When Bean admitted to her how hopeless he felt without Cynthia, Trish said cruelly, “Sometimes you’re unprotected from heat and light.”

One day, when Bean was at work, Cynthia came and got Fruitloop.

One day, he picked the lock to Cynthia’s apartment and sat on her toilet, his head in his hands, not thinking anything. He just missed her.

One day, he went to the Lusty and put quarters in the machine and when he saw the fin of her tattoo, he ran out.

He had let Fruitloop out into the yard, claiming her right to be feral. Of course she had gotten fleas. Almost every night, Bean lay on his stomach, at the edge of the library, and watched the fleas spring across the carpet. He imagined them astronauts bounding over moonrocks.

Sea of the Edge, Ocean of Storms, Marsh of Epidemics.

The Black Seed of Revelation

Bean tried to hold on to the rare moments when he could actually smell the air – the teardrops of jasmine, too much oil on someone else’s bike chain. It was those moments that helped him finally work up the nerve to tell Trish about the needle stick.

That morning, he heard Kirby’s horn, and he found Trish packing a duffelbag, and while worse things had happened to him, he couldn’t remember a time he felt so deflated. He fell limply onto her futon.

“What the hell?” he said.

“Near the Lost Coast, I think. Kirby’s uncle has a cabin on

the Bear River."

"For how long?"

"Four or five days."

"I don't want to be alone here," he said. "How the hell do I get out from under this cloud?"

"Frustration is the black seed of revelation."

"Sometimes you sound like you're reading tarot, you know that?"

"You could try gratitude," she said.

It was the first time that he had ever heard sarcasm in her voice.

Kirby honked again. His horn sounded like a clown's nose.

Tulips, zinnias, and dark roses sat in mason jars on Trish's windowsill. Bean stood up. "I'll water these for you," he said. "Do you want me to water them?"

Trish wrapped her arms around the small of his back. "You're so silly," she whispered. "They're dried."

She went down the stairs.

"I knew that," he said.

"Even when I'm super upset with you," she said, "I love you."

Trish shut the front door. Bean stayed on her futon. Exactly what was he grateful for? The toy train at Tilden, the new Peruvian restaurant on Shattuck. Grains of quinoa as big as fingernails. Grateful for Callie. Grateful for Dave, whose hands smelled of dough. And for NEED. Even if he was dying, he could commit to the long haul, helping others as long as his flesh would allow. And he was most grateful for Trish, who hadn't given up on him. She lit *Virgen de Guadalupe* prayer candles in his room when he slept, moved the empty bottles of King Cobra further from the bed.

Peeling an Egg

The buzz of the alarm clock made him feel intensely sad. The melted twists in the handle of the crockpot itched at his hands. Even the hard-boiled eggs, a morning ritual that usually calmed him, felt far away.

He turned on the stove – click, click, click. As the water boiled, he fumigated the library, setting the spray cans and closing the door behind him.

Normally, once the eggs were done, he would put them in a bowl to cool. He would rattle the bowl, pretending that the little ones were hatching. But he didn't have time. He had to get to the free clinic, then straight to NEED.

To keep his hand from burning, Bean rolled the two hot eggs around on his palm, like those balls he got for his birthday last year, something Chinese, something with an apostrophe. Supposedly they made a melody when moved in the right way.

An apostrophe might be a failure mechanism; a tiny mark to prove that something else had once lived there.

Bean blew on the eggs before peeling them. He started peeling at the tropics. Cancer, Capricorn.

If the tropics were lined with gold filament, as on a globe.

The shell, hopelessly stuck to the egg white, came off in shards.

Once Trish said, "The greater the number of fragments, the more loose strands of a life."

"If it all comes out in one long string," she said, "one is quicksanded in self-delusion."

With his front teeth, Bean gnawed off the top of the egg.

Chipmunk doing a craniotomy, he thought. Yellow sun, pasty eye, blister luck.

Bean? Hello? Eat the fucking egg and get on with it.

7.

Much Later

Trish, sitting cross-legged on an outcrop overlooking Tassajara Creek, will write:

Kirby didn't take my mouth from me. He took my hands. Not having an outlet for my voice turned hands into writing implements. When something is purely mechanical, it threatens to lose the parts of itself that exceed gravity.

Here I use my hands mulching the garden.

Here the lavender grows like peacock tails. Bees flit and hover at the stems.

Time now told by lights and drums and bells. The oil lamps lit at 5AM. Slippers on the raked dirt in front of my cabin. 30 minutes later someone runs through the monastery ringing a bell. Maybe it's a triangle. Sometimes before sun there's birds. Yesterday a blue jay by the dining room sat next to me on the bench. Then the wooden drum. Then the old wooden gong struck by old wooden block. Ten minutes.

The space between big toe and second toe is calloused from my slippers.

Sometimes a frog sits on the river-smooth rock by my lantern. If I've slept poorly or not dreamed – different than not remembering a dream – I stick out my tongue at it.

Sometimes people gather around the hot water machine. They hold their teacups. The boiling water in the metal box sounds like hammering dents from fenders. The smell of coffee and sometimes chamomile. Rosemary, which in dark gives out more scent.

The stars are innumerable and close.

The air before sunrise smells thick. I feel my nostrils expand towards the soil. Ten beats of the drum, decreasing intervals. Running water – washing of hands before entering the zendo. Trying not to creak the floorboards. Trying is trying too hard. By the next set of claps of wood on wood I'm settled on my zafu. I don't bow to the photo of the roshi and the sprigged flowers and the candle because I haven't yet learned reverence. Trust takes time to return. Sometimes long robes drag the pebbles along. The bones of my pelvis adjust weight on the zafu. I shoo off the dust from the zambutan. The breathing of those around me, fogging up this now. I half-close my eyes. The clearest bell sound of a mallet hitting a pitched bowl.

Perfect is the heat of this rock in my palm.

The sound of the gong ripples through the zendo. Sound in slow waves like a rock plunked into a pond. It says time is always now. I can't help thinking of the boy falling off Niagara Falls in a barrel. Dissolving like a water bubble into froth.

Let the thought fall.

It says come back to the breath. It says come back.

After breakfast, after my dishwashing duties, I scoop my hands into the garden. I remember making this motion as a child, the wet sand of Oregon. I feel how my fingertips touch the moist dirt, and how it crumbles as I push down, and how I lift it up to aerate it. Often there's a pillbug or worm in the clods of what will one day be lettuce.

I say to the creatures, "Good Morning."

Some days I pretend I'm the worm, pushing my finger into the loam of a nectarine.

Some days I feel myself grow softer, more pliant.

I followed a rattlesnake 40 steps down the path to the supply room. For only a second was I sad when it slithered into the creosote, and then I was something else.

THANKS

While there's usually one name on the cover of a book of fiction, it is, in no uncertain terms, a collective affair. In this light, I give unending thanks to everyone at C&R for your support, for so many insightful eyes and ears. To my parents, Howard and Linda, and to my sister Beth, much love, and my deepest appreciation for the tools to extend my own vectors. I couldn't have started this project without Debra Monroe, who convinced me that I could write, and Laura Carmichael, with whom many of these stories germinated. Early stages of this manuscript took shape in the *gezellig* confines of Amsterdam, under the sign of *Versal*: Jennifer Arcuni, Anna Arov, BJ Hollars, Kai Lashley, Bonnie J. Rough, and especially Megan M. Garr. My extended graduate cohort in Salt Lake City helped fashion these stories in immeasurable ways: Cami Nelson, Barbara Duffey, Matthew Kirkpatrick, dawn lonsinger, Susan McCarty, and April Wilder, as well as the faculty who pushed, who challenged: Scott Black, Karen Brennan, Francois Camoin, Lance Olsen, and Melanie Rae Thon. For deep-cut reading and deep-cut friendship, I owe extra-special gratitude to Halina Duraj, Rachel Marston, and Shena McAuliffe. Jacob Paul, your incisiveness and generosity was instrumental in getting me over the line. Geoff Babbitt, Kathryn Cowles, Megan Kaminski, Esther Lee, Rebecca Lindenberg, Tim O'Keefe, Jessie Sholl: thank you for your friendship, your intensities. I received financial support from the Steffensen Cannon Scholarship at the University of Utah, for which I am grateful. And lastly, to Anne M. Royston, whose love and smarts mean everything, day after day.

C&R PRESS TITLES

NONFICTION

Women in the Literary Landscape by Doris Weatherford, et al

Credo: An Anthology of Manifestos & Sourcebook for Creative Writing by Rita Banerjee and Diana Norma Szokolyai

FICTION

Made by Mary by Laura Catherine Brown

Ivy vs. Dogg by Brian Leung

While You Were Gone by Sybil Baker

Cloud Diary by Steve Mitchell

Spectrum by Martin Ott

That Man in Our Lives by Xu Xi

SHORT FICTION

Notes From the Mother Tongue by An Tran

The Protester Has Been Released by Janet Sarbanes

ESSAY AND CREATIVE NONFICTION

Immigration Essays by Sybil Baker
Je suis l'autre: Essays and Interrogations by Kristina Marie Darling
Death of Art by Chris Campanioni

POETRY

My Stunt Double by Travis Denton
Lessons in Camoflauge by Martin Ott
Dark Horse by Kristina Marie Darling
All My Heroes are Broke by Ariel Francisco
Holdfast by Christian Anton Gerard
Ex Domestica by E.G. Cunningham
Like Lesser Gods by Bruce McEver
Notes from the Negro Side of the Moon by Earl Braggs
Imagine Not Drowning by Kelli Allen
Notes to the Beloved by Michelle Bitting
Free Boat: Collected Lies and Love Poems by John Reed
Les Fauves by Barbara Crooker
Tall as You are Tall Between Them by Annie Christain
The Couple Who Fell to Earth by Michelle Bitting
Notes to the Beloved by Michelle Bitting

CPSIA information can be obtained
at www.ICGtesting.com
Printed in the USA
FSHW020033301019
63534FS

9 781949 540048